Love and Death in Tucson
A Love and Death Mystery & Political Espionage Novel

Volume 11

Hal Graff

Copyright © 2023 **Harold Graff II Publishing**

All rights reserved. No part of this publication may be reproduced, distributed, or transmitted in any form or by any means, including photocopying, recording, or other electronic or mechanical methods, without the prior written permission of the publisher, except in the case of brief quotations embodied in critical reviews and certain other noncommercial uses permitted by copyright law. For permission requests, write to the publisher, addressed "Attention: Book Rights and Permission," at the address below.

Published in the United States of America

ISBN 978-1-962569-28-6 (SC)
ISBN 978-1-962569-26-2 (HC)
ISBN 978-1-962569-27-9 (Ebook)

Harold Graff II Publishing
222 West 6th Street
Suite 400, San Pedro, CA, 90731
sec26para5@yahoo.com

Order Information and Rights Permission:

Quantity sales. Special discounts might be available on quantity purchases by corporations, associations, and others. For details, contact the publisher at the address above.

For Book Rights Adaptation and other Rights Permission. Call us at toll-free 1-888-945-8513 or send us an email at admin@stellarliterary.com.

*For Eric, Lainen, Colton, Ethan, Jenny, Scott,
Finn, and Kade*

*And for my Creator, my God in Heaven, my Lord and Savior,
Jesus Christ, my comforter, and guide, the Holy Spirit, and the
Holy Trinity*

WORKS BY DR. HAL GRAFF
(6,478,043 total published words)

The Love and Death Series
Harold Gatewood Mysteries
(Mystery / Political Espionage)

Love and Death at the Encierro Vol. 1
Love and Death in Cuba Vol. 2
Love and Death in Tokyo Vol. 3
Love and Death in Beijing Vol. 4
Love and Death in London Vol. 5
Love and Death in Korea Vol. 6
Love and Death in Venezuela Vol. 7
Love and Death in Mexico Vol. 8
Love and Death in the Dominican Republic Vol. 9
Love and Death: a Journey Vol. 10
Love and Death in Tuscon Vol. 11
The Harold Gatewood Mysteries: An Encyclopedia Vol. 12 (For my use only)
Love and Death in Virginia Vol. 13
Love and Death in Chile Vol. 14
Love and Death in Paris Vol.15
Love and Death in the Orient Vol. 16
Love and Death in the China Sea Vol. 17
Love and Death in Caracas Vol. 18
Love and Death in Chicago Vol. 19
Love and Death in Moscow Vol. 20
Love and Death in the Ukraine Vol. 21
Love and Death in Rome Vol. 22
The Harold Gatewood Mysteries: An Encyclopedia Vol. 2 (Vol. 2 is for my use only)
Love and Death in the British Isles Vol. 24
Love and Death in the Philippines Vol. 25
Love and Death in Barcelona Vol. 26
Gatewood Returns Vol. 27

The Davis Finn Mysteries
(Historical Fiction / Mystery / Political Espionage)

Murder in Georgia Vol. 1 (A Quadrilogy – Book 1)
Murder in Montana Vol. 2 (A Quadrilogy - Book 2)
Murder in the FBI Vol. 3 (A Quadrilogy – Book 3)
Murder in Vietnam Vol. 4 (A Quadrilogy – Book 4)
Angel of Mercy Vol. 5
Oxy Vol. 6 (A Trilogy – Book 1)
The White Duck Vol. 7 (A Trilogy – Book 2)
Sucker Punch Vol. 8 (A Trilogy – Book 3)
Eddy Vol. 9
Counterfeit Vol. 10 (A Trilogy – Book 1)
Montenegro Vol. 11 (A Trilogy – Book 2)
Triple Crown Vol. 12 (A Trilogy – Book 3)
Murder in Oxford Vol. 13 (A Trilogy – Book 1)
Revenge Vol. 14 (A Trilogy – Book 2)
Survival Vol. 15 (A Trilogy – Book 3)
The Mississippi Hangman Vol. 16 (A Trilogy – Book 1)
A Dead President Vol. 17 (A Trilogy – Book 2)
Oath of Office Vol. 18 (A Trilogy – Book 3)
Finn and Gatewood's Outdoor Adventures Vol. 19
Stockholm Syndrome Vol. 20 (A Trilogy – Book 1)
Blood Feud Vol. 21 (A Trilogy – Book 2)
A Terrible Tragedy Vol. 22 (A Trilogy – Book 3)
Takedown Vol.23
Blackmail Vol. 24
Dead Like Lincoln Vol. 25
Lethal Force Vol. 26
The Leopard Vol. 27
The Crossbow Killer Vol. 28
The Ten Pin Killer Vol. 29
The Grand Bargain Vol. 30
Jill Vol. 31 (A Trilogy – Book 1)
Double-cross Vol. 32 (A Trilogy – Book 2)
The Seven Iron Murders Vol.33 (A Trilogy – Book 3)
The Corner Pocket Killer Vol. 34

The Choke Hold Murders Vol. 36
The Midterm Elections Vol. 37
Death Dressed in Blue Vol. 38
His Better Half Vol. 39
Ten Little Indians Vol. 40 (A Trilogy – Book 1)
The Cassowary Vol. 41 (A Trilogy – Book 2)
Remember, Remember, the 5th Of November Vol. 42 (A Trilogy – Book 3)

The Parker Weston Romance, Action, Mysteries

Penelope Vol. 1 (A Trilogy – Book 1)
The Bad Boy Vol. 2 (A Trilogy – Book 2)
Tall Buffalo Vol. 3 (A Trilogy – Book 3)
1, 2, 3, 4, Enter Murder's Door Vol. 4 (A Trilogy – Book 1)
The Sky's the Limit, John Vol. 5 (A Trilogy – Book 2)
Love Will Keep Us Together Vol. 6 (A Trilogy – Book 3)

The Bobby Ross Faith Series

Bobby Ross and the White Stones Vol. 1

The Aidan Conall Mysteries

Carnage at Harvard Vol. 1 (A Trilogy – Book 1)
Its Forty – Love Vol. 2 (A Trilogy – Book 2)
Its Match Point Vol. 3 (A Trilogy – Book 3)

Disclaimer

This story is a work of fiction. The names of characters, their actions, locations, events, situations, organizations, companies, religious or ethnic groups, story line, and any other item in this fictional work are the result of my creation. Any likeness to the areas mentioned above, or people living, or who have passed away, is accidental and was not used for any harmful purpose in this work of fiction.

Table of Contents

Prologue xi
Chapter 1 The Cards 1
Chapter 2 Follow Through 7
Chapter 3 Ready To Sting 17
Chapter 4 There Was Plenty To Go Around 22
Chapter 5 "This time my friends" 25
Chapter 6 "For Sofia" 34
Chapter 7 Operacion Para Romper 43
Chapter 8 A New Man 48
Chapter 9 "I love my new profession" 59
Chapter 10 The ANNM 73
Chapter 11 The Same Alley 77
Chapter 12 The Trip North 80
Chapter 13 A Sailor 84
Chapter 14 Addiction 87
Chapter 15 The Wild, Wild West 95
Chapter 16 No Capital Punishment 98
Chapter 17 The Rodeo 101
Chapter 18 Season Opener 104
Chapter 19 The Fountain of Youth 107
Chapter 20 "It will work" 110

Chapter 21 "A fine day for a walk" 113
Chapter 22 No Net Gain 116
Chapter 23 The Return... 118
Chapter 24 "I will"... 122
Chapter 25 Failure.. 127
Chapter 26 The Call 129
Chapter 27 Vudu.. 133

Prologue

CHRISTMAS AND NEW YEARS had come and gone, and Harold Gatewood had decided that life in Gibson City was good once again. Day by day, he had forgotten the events in the Dominican Republic and started to think about his future, and his baseball comeback.

He had enjoyed the safety of his small home town, and the close relationship with his family. After his first week back home, during which he had locked the doors and shut out the world to recover, his friends started to call and visit. His good friend Thomas Jares, who had helped him in the past, was the first person allowed to visit.

Two days later Jares had surprised Harold with his good friends from Foosland and Elliott. Their visit was a shot in the arm for Harold, as he had laughed for the first time in many days. Later, his minister had stopped by and talked for over an hour. He felt like he was free of the terrible memories of the incidents in the Dominican Republic and started to work out again.

He knew he might backslide and let the hideous memories of the events of the Dominican Republic reenter his mind, but for now he was free.

He had reflected on his time since he had first become injured and was banished from baseball, thrown out on the trash heap of washed-up ballplayers who would never return to their beloved profession.

Since that day he had been through a lifetime of horrors. He had gone to San Toro de Lidia, Spain and battled with the Abertzale Indepentzia Oaintze, the AIO terrorist organization that had become the main threat in his life. They had continued to dog him to this very day. They had followed him to Cuba, where he had escaped their assassin's bullets and had become embroiled in the attempted coup of the Cuban government.

He had then returned to baseball in his first comeback attempt, playing for the Central Illinois Magicians. His short stop with the Magicians was marked with success and he was sold to the Tokyo Cardinals in Japan. Fate led him to face the powerful Yakaza crime family.

His next stop on the comeback trail was in Beijing, China were he was ticketed for extinction by the Yakaza and the AIO once again. Not to admit defeat in their attempts, both the Yakaza and the AIO continued their missions to kill him when he moved on to play for the Seoul Cranes, in South Korea.

He had escaped with his life and made his successful return to major league baseball with the Miami Raiders. His return was short-lived as his evil demon, injury, again snuffed out his career.

Out of baseball once again, and deemed finished as a ballplayer, he moved on to Venezuela where he battled the evil Nazoa government, the Columbian drug cartels, the True Columbian People's Liberation Movement, a Venezuelan mob with Sicilian roots, and the AIO. His next stop was in Mexico City where he encountered the corrupt Mexican government of Alto Roble, the drug cartel leader, and once again, the AIO.

His next "wonderful vacation spot location" was the Dominican Republic. He renewed his exploits with the Nazoa government, the Columbian drug cartels, the TCPLM, the Venezuelan mafia, and the AIO. He also added the Sicilian mafia, out of Palermo, to the list of people who wanted his head as a trophy.

Along the way, he had become a contract agent for America's Central Information Organization. He had performed marvelously for the CIO and had protected America's interests in the stops from San Toro De Lidia, Spain to the Dominican Republic. He had also killed for them, in the line of duty.

Now, he was home again in Gibson City, hoping never to deal with his long list of enemies again. He wanted to concentrate on playing baseball, and defeating Father Time in his comeback attempt.

He had been written off as a player long ago, and in the vernacular of 1930's humor, was deader than Kelsey's nuts as a baseball player. He was now just a speck of dust on the scrapheap of past baseball careers.

But, Gatewood had a surprise in store for major league baseball, a big surprise.

Chapter 1

The Cards

January 18

THE TAROT CARDS NEVER LIE. She was a large, heavy-set woman clad in a long white-colored skirt, bright turquoise-blue-colored blouse, and leather sandals. She wore large hooped-shaped earrings that dangled from her ears like anvils.

As she sat, she talked with her son, Manuel. She then proceeded to place four cards, one at each corner in a square-like pattern on the table in front of her. She then added a fifth card in the middle of the square. She thought, and remembered the first time she had seen him in the Dominican Republic.

He had walked along the street from his hotel room, window-shopping and gawking like the typical tourist to the island. She had laughed at him, as he looked like a fish out of water. He had stopped at the park and struck up a conversation with the old men who were playing dominoes, trying to learn the basics of the game, and attempting to pick up any information about the movement of cocaine originating in Columbia and shipped from the island to North America.

She had watched him approach her, noticing his athletic build, handsome looks, and infectious smile. She remembered their first conversation. She had been the first to speak, saying, I know why you are here."

The first words he had said to her were, "I am sorry Mam. I did not hear what you said."

"I said that I know why you are here."

Gatewood had thought, "I'll bite." He then said, "Why am I here?"

"You are here to find baseball players."

Amazed with what he had heard, he had said, "How do you know that?"

"The spirits told me."

"Mam, it was in the newspaper that I was coming here to do that."

"The spirits do not read the newspaper."

"What spirits?"

"Dominican Vudu spirits."

"Really?"

"Yes. They tell me what lies ahead for you."

"What is that?"

"You face danger from your enemies, old and new."

"How would you help me?"

"I will call upon Belie Belcan, our patron saint of justice and protection, to watch over your safety."

"Why would you do that?"

"Because that is my mission in life. I use my religion, vudu, to protect people who will come to believe in its magic."

"What will that cost me?"

"Nothing. I am in what your religion calls a guardian angel."

He had said, "I am not convinced."

"That is what all skeptics say. You will also face danger tonight."

"How will that happen?"

"It will come from an unexpected direction."

"I thank you for your concern Mam but I am just having supper with a friend tonight."

"Danger lurks my son."

"I thank you for your input Mam. I must return now as I have things to do."

"Yes, return to room one hundred."

"How did you know that?"

"It is a very easy question to answer."

Gatewood thought, "It is common knowledge that I always ask for room one hundred."

"I will see you again my son. You will be back. Do not be afraid. I will help protect you."

Harold had thanked the lady and walked back to his hotel to get ready for his date with Linda Westmorland. After showering, and getting ready for his date, he walked to the elevator and pushed the number six. As he rode up to the sixth floor he thought, "What silliness. I am only meeting Linda. She did not seem dangerous to me."

The old woman, Gatewood's vudu guardian angel, laughed at her recollection of their first conversation, and remembered what had happened when they had next met. He had spoken first that time.

"Hello my guardian angel. What is in store for me, according to your vudu magic?"

"Harold, do not tease me about serious things. You will be a believer soon."

"You may be right."

"Do you have any questions for me?"

"Yes. Why do you in the Dominican spell vudu with the letter u, rather than how we do it in America, with the letter o?"

"We do because we are believers. It is a religion we follow. To you Americans it is something to snicker at, and to enjoy in the movies. It is serious to us, and we spell it the way our ancestors did."

"Thank you for the history lesson. And, with due respect to your beliefs, I now understand."

"Harold, do you have any other questions for me?"

"No. Do you have a question for me my dear lady?"

"Yes, I do."

"Please tell me what it is so I can answer it and head back to my hotel. I am tired."

"My good friend, would you like to go to a cockfight this evening?"

Gatewood was shocked back into reality by the question. This was the contact who had written the letter to him mentioning that he would meet a person who could put him in contact with the cartel employees in the Dominican who were shipping the drugs to North America.

"I can tell you are surprised Mr. Gatewood."

"Please tell me what you meant by your note."

"I meant everything in the note. I can help you deal with the drug shipments in and out of the country. They come from Columbia, through Venezuela, and are housed here until they are flown into the United States and Canada. They have been doing it for years. My fellow worshipers do not like the drug trade as it has been a blotch on our country's culture and reputation for many years."

"How did you know to contact me with this information?"

"I know you are working for the CIO again Harold. I read it in the vudu cards."

"Are you going to take me there?"

"No. My sole surviving son will pick you up at your motel at eight-thirty and drive you to the cockfight, which starts at nine-fifteen."

"I will be ready, and in the lobby."

"He will be driving a black, four-door, Russian-made compact car. His name is Manuel. He will point out the people at the cockfight that work for the cartel. You can take pictures of them tonight, when they are busy watching the fight. Manuel will also tell you about each of them so your CIO can monitor their movements and decide how to use them to help slow down the drug trade through our country."

"Please tell me again why you and your son do this type of work. I know that there is another reason besides your beliefs."

"You are smart for an American Harold. I lost my oldest two sons to the drug trade. One was hooked on cocaine and overdosed. The other was killed when the cartel caught him nosing around one of their drop sites. He was careless and it cost him his life. Do not be careless around the drug cartel Harold."

"I am sorry for the loss of your two sons. I will try to make them pay for what they have done to your family."

"I was hoping you would help us in that area. My family will be most appreciative of your efforts."

"I will be ready when Manuel arrives at the hotel tonight."

"One more thing Harold. Are you being careful? You know that I told you people want you dead and there is trouble, and death, in your future."

"I understand now. The cartels are a threat to me."

"That is correct. But the cards tell me death could come from three other sources. Please be careful."

"Three sources?"

"Yes. Be careful."

Harold thanked his guardian angel and headed to his last stop of the day.

The old woman's comments about three sources being after him had been proven right. Today, she remembered her warning, laughed and looked at her son. She then said, "What do you remember about him?"

Her son, Manuel, replied, "I remember that you had me take him to a cockfight to meet the drug cartel employees here on the island.'

Harold had ridden the elevator from his hotel room downstairs. He had waited for ten minutes and had seen Manuel pull up in front of the hotel. He had walked to the car, hopped in, and they had sped off to their destination, the cockfight.

Harold had witnessed cockfights before. In the Dominican Republic, cockfighting was almost as popular as baseball. Manuel had briefed Harold on how the cartel had killed his two brothers, one by violence and one by hooking him on drugs.

He explained that the vudu religion opposed the carnage the cartel had brought to the island, and how their members had watched the deliveries and flights out to North America, cataloged the times and locations, and forwarded the information to the CIO. The recent increase in shipments was caused by the cartel changing its routes and eliminating vudu "snitches" like his brother who had killed.

Manuel had asked, "Have you ever lost someone you loved to the cartels?"

Harold thought of Luisa Gaicia and said, "Yes. I loved a woman who was killed by the cartels."

"Then you know how I feel. I want to kill every cartel member I can."

They had finished the forty-five minute drive from Harold's hotel to the barn where the birds would fight. The fighting roosters lived a pampered life, being especially bred to bring out their special fighting traits like aggressiveness, stamina, and strength. Harold remembered a similar discussion with Aitor Lehoi and Gabriel Domeka when Aitor proudly discussed how he had developed a special strain of Iberian fighting bulls for the bullring in San Toro de Lidia.

Before entering the barn Manuel reviewed what Gatewood should do before, during, and after the fights. He told Harold, "Be quiet, listen for helpful information, take pictures without being noticed, and bet on the fights. You will need to bet exactly as I do. Besides getting helpful information, we might win a few pesos tonight."

The appearance of the fighting roosters were as Harold had remembered them, adorned with a large bulbous knot, called a comb, on their heads and a wattle, called a carnacle, hanging from their head or neck. The carnacles reminded Harold of those on the turkey species he had hunted in several places in the world. He had earned the world slam designation of turkey hunting, killing an Eastern in Michigan, a Merriam in Wyoming, a Rio Grande in Texas, an Osceola in Florida, and a Gould and an Ocellated in Mexico.

Other bird species also displayed carnacles, including pheasants, condors, falcons, vultures, eagles, storks, spoonbills, swans, geese, cuckoos, cockatoos, and the Muscovy duck, which he had seen in Mexico.

The roosters had spurs tied or taped to their legs, and were paired in their contest by weight. Before the contest would start the owners and handlers would bring each bird out, raise it above their head and parade around the circular ring where the birds would fight, called a valla. The purpose served to display the birds, whip the crowd into a frenzied state, and increase the betting and the odds on each bird.

The fight usually lasted one round, typically lasting around five minutes. Injuries or death could take place due to the sharp spurs on the contestants' legs.

Harold had used the evening to gather information on the cartel members that he would forward to CIO headquarters in Washington, D.C. He also had a wonderful time, screaming and yelling for his rooster of choice in each contest. By the time Manuel and he had left they had amassed a fair amount of earnings from their betting skills as the stakes were always high.

When they reached the hotel Harold had thanked Manuel for his help and promised he would help bring revenge on the cartel for what they had done to his brothers. He then asked a question, "How will we stay in touch?"

Manuel had replied, "Visit my mother each day as you have been." She would arrange any meeting that was needed, and she would pass along information that would help his efforts. If we would work together closely we should be able to obtain some good results.

The old woman looked again at the tarot cards. She first turned over the top, left-cornered card in the square pattern on the table and asked, "Who is he?" She turned over the card that pictured the King of Sceptres. She said, "He is a country gentleman, a good man, with knowledge and education."

She then turned over the card on the lower, left-cornered square, and asked, "What will he do?" The card was the Six of Swords. She said, "He leaves on a voyage."

She then turned over the top card on the right side of the square and asked, "Where does he go?" The card was the Ten of Cups. She said, "He goes to a place of combat, opposition, and dispute."

She then turned over the lower card on the left side of the square and asked, "What awaits?" The card showed the Devil. She said, "Evil awaits."

She turned over the last card in the middle of the square. She asked, "What is the result?" The card was the death card. She said, "Death is the result."

The old woman, with a look of concern and fear on her face, spoke again. "Harold Gatewood, the tarot cards have foretold your future. You need to heed their warnings and be careful. Combat, opposition, and dispute will be your constant companions, and death will be the result. The cards never lie."

Chapter 2

Follow Through

February 18

THE SNOW WAS UP TO GATEWOOD'S mid-thigh as he trudged from his workout building to his house. It had been a cold, snowy Winter and Gatewood was ready for some sunshine. He sat down in his chair in the living room and thought about being in Illinois in mid-February.

Pitchers and catchers were just reporting to Spring training and the baseball season was just a few weeks away. He had worked hard at his conditioning program and knew he was almost ready for his long-shot comeback attempt. He needed a team that would give him an opportunity as Randle Quinn, his agent, had not found a team who was willing to even give him a tryout.

Gatewood relaxed and let his mind wander to other matters. He wondered if Leal Servidor, the Mexican president, was still making progress in his attempts to change events in his country. Gatewood remembered Servidor's comments when they had first met.

Servidor had described how Luisa Gaicia had performed in her work as his children's nanny. His two children, a boy six and a girl aged five, had been playing in the park in Mexico City. They both had called for Luisa to push them in the swings. Both children had laughed as they ascended to what seemed like the top of the sky when their swing was pushed forward. When they made the return trip downward they were lifted up in their swings by their nanny, and pushed forward again, back to what they again though was the apex of the sky.

Luisa had laughed with the children as they enjoyed each back-and-forth trip of the swing. She loved being with the children in a safe location and a pleasant setting. She had worked at her job for three weeks and felt as though she had been given a reprieve from the recent horrors of her life. The children had provided an enjoyable break from her journey to America and the job had provided a small salary in addition to her free room and board.

Her employer and wife were nice. She had felt fortunate to be working for a loving family. The husband held a high governmental position, and the wife was a socialite from Mexico City. She had met her employers when she was sitting in the same park where she was now swinging the children. The wife had noticed how the Luisa's pleasant personality had immediately won over the children that first day they had accidentally met in the park.

She had been hired immediately, and started to work the next day. She was thankful the couple had not required any references or citizenship evidence, as she was one of the many illegal immigrants passing through the country Northward toward America, and a better life.

She was part of a large staff, and due to her hard work, had fit in well with her coworkers. She watched the children during the day while the mother was involved in her duties as the wife of the vice-president of the country. She was thankful the couple had provided a clothing allowance for her position, as she was expected to be clean, and presentable, in her position, as she might be seen or photographed with the children and needed to provide a dignified presence to the public, as it reflected on her employer, Vice-President Leal Servidor.

Her beauty had attracted many admirers in her short career, but she only had eyes for one man, Harold Gatewood. She did not know he was in Mexico City, and had still planned on making her way to the border, and crossing into America. She also had not known that Gatewood was now at another low point in his life, as he had just shot and killed a woman, Adriana Izar, at the bullfights when he had been attacked by AIO hitman Sandalio La Muerte.

The couple was moving in a parallel universe, living not three miles apart, yet not knowing the other was near. Gatewood had gone through police questioning after the attack and shooting incident. He had been cleared of any charges on the basis of self-defense. Yet, he was a man in the depths of despair, as he had killed someone close to him, and felt responsible.

The incident had taken place the week before, but he was still reliving the situation on a constant basis. He had tried to work, but at the ballpark, his mind seldom left the incident. On some days, he had gone to scout a ballgame, and found himself back in his hotel room, without one memory of anything he had seen or done the entire day.

She had not known that Gatewood had been invited to meet the vice-president, a wild baseball fan, but he had rescheduled due to the incident. He had been invited again and had realized he needed to return to the real world, and that the honor of meeting the vice-president would be good for his spirits. He had been picked up by Leal Servidor's personal staff, taken to the personal quarters for lunch, and then returned to his hotel.

Gatewood smiled as he remembered how he had looked at himself in the mirror of his hotel room. He had been urged to dress casually, and had opted for tan slacks, a light blue shirt adorned with a navy-blue tie that was completed in a perfect Windsor-knot fashion, a navy-blue sport coat, brown slip-on shoes, and brown socks. He had mustered a smile on to his face and completed his inspection. He had thought, "I may not feel one hundred percent, but at least I look the part."

After being squired to the personal quarters in the official government vehicle, Gatewood had relaxed in a waiting room. After ten minutes, he had been greeted by the vice-president, and they had engaged in pleasant conversation, which he remembered verbatim.

"Harold, it is nice to meet you."

"Thank you for inviting me. It is an honor to meet you Sir."

"Harold, please call me Leal."

"Thank you. I will."

"Good. We are friends so please be informal."

"I will."

"You have been here several weeks. What do you think of our city?"

"I have enjoyed my time here. The city is diverse, has many cultural activities, and is a very beautiful place to live."

"I am glad you like it. How much longer will you be staying?"

"I will scout at least through the end of the season unless they pull me out to place me on a special assignment elsewhere."

"Have you uncovered some prospects?"

"Yes, there are several promising players here who have a baseball future."

"I have loved baseball from when I was a young boy. But, I was not blessed with baseball skills. I live vicariously through other's exploits."

"It is a great game. Like you, it is part of my life. I couldn't have envisioned my life without baseball."

"You played a long time Harold, and you had a great career."

"Thank you."

"Your comeback was inspirational to many people, including me."

"That is nice of you to say Leal."

"It is true. How are you feeling?"

"Do you mean after the incident last week?"

"Yes."

"I am shaken but I am stable now. It is tough to accidentally shoot someone for whom you have strong feelings."

"I can only guess how you are feeling. If I lost my wife and children I would be devastated."

"You have two children correct?"

"Yes, a son and a daughter."

"You are a blessed man."

"Yes. My wife and children are my life."

Harold thought about the killing of his wife Akemi and their unborn son Tai. After a long silence he said, "I am sure they are the most important part of your life Leal."

"Harold, I have always wanted to see a baseball game in the United States."

"You should come to watch several games, perhaps one in every park in both leagues."

"That would be very enjoyable."

"Please let me know if you want to see a game. I will make a couple calls for you and they can roll out the red carpet."

"I would rather go to the park incognito. That way I could eat a hot dog and not worry about spilling mustard on my shirt, or having a beer and not worrying about spilling it on myself. The press would have a field day if that happened."

"Perhaps you could make that trip happen when you become president of the country."

"I do plan on becoming president one day."

"I hope you do."

"I want to improve relations with the United States. I will shut down the cartels. Their violence, drug smuggling, and ushering illegal immigrants to the border of our countries can't be tolerated."

Harold had not believed what he had just heard. He had been asked by the CIO to be observant and pick up information about the situation in the Mexican government and the comments sounded sincere. If Servidor could become president relations would improve dramatically. He had thought that could not wait to tell Rick Owens about the vice-president's comments.

"Leal, what can be done about the cartels?"

"I have an opposing outlook and different goals than the man I currently assist in the government, Alto Roble. When it comes to relations with America, and the areas I mentioned, we are at other ends of the spectrum. I don't support his actions. I will change them if I can lead Mexico in the future."

"That would be very beneficial for both of our countries."

"It is a change that needs to be made. For now, my hands are tied."

The conversation had been interrupted by Leal's son and daughter. They had run into the dining area, thrown their hands around him, kissed him, laughed, and told him they loved him. He returned the affection and had said to a woman standing behind Gatewood, "Hello, please take the children to the living quarters."

The woman had walked forward, taken the children's hands and had started to walk away. She was stopped, and Leal had said, "I would like you to meet someone. This is Harold Gatewood, a great baseball player from America."

The nanny had looked at the man and had then stood in disbelief. Harold had raised his eyes from his plate and had also entered a state of disbelief. Leal had continued, "Harold, this is our nanny, Ms. Luisa Gaicia."

Luisa and Harold had looked at each other in silence for a long moment. Finally, Harold had gathered his thoughts, stood up, placed his napkin on the table, and somehow had sputtered out the words, "Miss Gaicia, it is my honor to meet you."

Luisa had stood in silence as their eyes concentrated on each other. Everything else in the world was blacked out, and only the fact that they were actually looking at each other mattered. She had struggled to speak, and choked out the words, "Thank you Mr. Gatewood. It is my honor to meet you also."

Harold had then extended his right hand. Luisa, had reached out, touched it, and placed her hand inside his. Magnetism had flown through the air as the couple stood holding hands for a long moment, not speaking, but only looking into each other's eyes.

Leal had broken atmosphere of the confusing situation and said, "That was quite an introduction. Do you two know each other?"

Harold had replied, "No, but is my honor to meet such a wonderful and beautiful woman. I understand you are the world's greatest nanny."

Luisa had smiled and laughed, and said, "Thank you for the nice compliment Mr. Gatewood."

Neither one of the couple had wanted their association known by anyone, especially the vice-president of the country. She was an illegal immigrant in Mexico, one whom thought she had killed a man in Caracas, Columbia, and was now working for the second most powerful politician in Mexico without any identification or citizenship. He was an ex-ballplayer who was working undercover as a spy for the CIO, and a person had had just killed his girlfriend after being attacked by an international terrorist hitman of the AIO. If the associations became public an international scandal would break loose.

Luisa had smiled, then excused herself, and took the children to the personal living quarters.

Leal had then spoken, "Harold, are you sure you do not know Luisa?"

"I do not know her, but I would like to. Would you do me a big favor and give her my phone number? Here is my cell phone number, and here is my hotel phone number. My room number is one hundred."

"I will. Room one hundred. I have read that you always ask for the room number. Is it your lucky number?"

"It certainly is Leal."

The two men had finished their meal, talked for twenty more minutes, then shook hands. Harold had been driven back his hotel. He had thanked his driver, gottten out of his car, had stood still for a moment, and had thanked God for the fact he had met Luisa again.

Across the street, on a roof top of a tall building, a man in a ghillie suit had been laying sprawled out on the roof. He had been waiting for three hours, and had been on the roof even before the government vehicle had picked up Gatewood for the luncheon with Leal. He would have killed Harold when he had walked out, said hello to the driver, and entered the car, but the driver had moved in front of Gatewood, obstructing the shooter's line of fire.

At the time, Sandalio La Muerte had cursed the driver's movement as it had prevented from his one-shot, one-kill plan to separate Gatewood from his earthly presence. Two times previously in the week since his attack on Gatewood at the bull ring, his assassination plans had been foiled by citizens entering into his line of fire.

Both times, Gatewood had exited the ballpark, looking like he was in a daze, and unaware of where he was. His guard had been down, and La Muerte had lost three easy opportunities to kill him. This time, it would happen. Gatewood stood in the middle of the sidewalk, looking in the shooter's direction, unaware of the assassin's presence on the roof.

La Muerte had sighed in his rifle, aimed it at the area between Gatewood's eyes, and envisioned his cartridge flying through the air and striking the victim in the kill zone. Vindication would be his as soon as he squeezed the trigger. A forefinger had squeezed the trigger and a round was sent toward its target. A thud was heard as the bullet entered the head between the eyes, tore through the front of the forehead, entered the brain, and expanded, shattering bone and brain tissue on its path through the back of the head.

The victim laid dead, his blood spilling out of the wound. Darren Fuller, the CIO operative who had been assigned to shadow Gatewood in Mexico, smiled and said, "That's one for the good guys." He then broke down his sniper rifle, packed it in its case, removed his ghillie suit, placed it in a black garbage bag, and headed down the back stairs of the hotel roof top, his protection duty completed for the evening.

Gatewood, clueless of what had happened, had turned and walked into the hotel lobby, rode the elevator to the first floor above the mezzanine level, entered his room, number one hundred, waited for a phone call, and said, "Yes, room one hundred has been lucky for me this time."

Luisa Gaicia had taken the two Servidor children to their mother, and had rushed to her personal quarters to call the number on the business card. She had said that she could not wait to speak to Harold.

Gatewood leaned back in his chair and took a deep breath as the memories had brought back many emotions. Harold owed a great deal to Leal Servidor as he had helped him find Luisa. The Servidor family had come to the Mexico City airport to see Luisa and he leave when they had returned to America.

Gatewood had then headed to the Dominican Republic and had followed Servidor's presidential decisions. Harold respected Leal Servidor, as he would ascended to the Mexican presidency when his predecessor, Alto Roble, had apparently died in a murder-suicide with two female companions aboard his yacht.

The fallout from the event had been massive as the ugliness of Roble's lifestyle of drugs and philandering made it to the front pages of the world's newspapers. Scandal and embarrassment had become Roble's legacy and Mexico's shame.

The Robe situation had made Servidor's transition into Mexico's leadership position difficult. The difference in Roble's lifestyle and his own could not have been clearer. Personally, he had nothing in common with Roble. Frankly, he despised the man because of his conduct, lack of morals, and his absence of a belief in God.

Leal was a devoted family man, had married his grade school sweetheart, was active in his church, and had lived his life in an honorable manner. He had entered politics at the local level, winning a seat on the school board, and then being elected mayor of his small home town in the most Northwestern state of Mexico.

He had won his first term in the Chamber of Disputes, the Camara de Diputados, at age twenty-six. He soon won the respect of his peers and was elected speaker of body at age thirty.

His choice as vice-president had been done in an attempt to take the pressure off Roble's pattern of corruption, personal habits, his ties to the drug cartels, and his antagonistic attitude toward Mexico's biggest trade partner, the United States.

Servidor hated the drug cartels. He had lost his younger brother to drugs provided by the cartel owned by Slavado Masas, the El Avispon Picante, the "stinging hornet". His father had been a businessman, operating a feed and hardware store. The elder Servidor had been forced to pay protection money to the Masas cartel. His mother had worked at the local library. Both were now deceased. Leal had come from good stock.

Servidor had sat in his office and thought about how he had been chosen to become the vice-president. He had been as surprised as everyone else when he had been picked out of the blue for the position. His being on the ticket was a counterbalance and a breath of fresh air to the poisoned atmosphere of the Roble administration.

Leal had sent a note of condolences to Harold Gatewood when Luisa had been killed. He had waited and had felt that enough time had passed for Gatewood to deal with the grief of her passing, and had called him at his cell number. Harold remembered their conversation.

"Hello, his is Harold Gatewood."

"Harold, this is Leal Servidor."

"Hello. It is nice to hear from you. How are you?"

"I am fine. Actually, I am calling to see how you are doing."

"Thank you. I am making progress."

"I wanted to call and tell you how sorry my family and I are about Luisa's death."

"Thank you."

"We all loved her. She was a kind, loving soul. My children miss her terribly. She was so wonderful with them."

Harold had said, "Thank you. She brought sunshine into everyone's lives."

"My children have had a hard time adjusting to her passing."

"I hope they are doing better."

"Thank you. We explain to them that Luisa is in heaven and smiling on them."

"Luisa had told me how grateful she had been for you hiring her as the children's nanny. She said that she loved you all very much. She had cried when she had to leave them when we flew back to America."

"Thank you. She was very special and quickly became part of our family."

"Yes she was. How are you doing Leal?"

"The transition has been rough sledding. I have been surprised by the scope of my new position. It looks much easier from the outside than what it is once a person has the job. There is much more to it but once you focus and prioritize what is needed it becomes manageable."

"You will do well because you are a good man."

"Thank you Harold. You are a good man also. You have done much to help Mexico by helping bring focus on Roble and the cartels."

"Thank you. We Americans are thankful you are now in office as our countries can now work together much more effectively. We all look forward to working with you."

"Thank you. We all need to put aside past differences and work on the areas where we can make progress. We need to stop the march of illegal immigrants flowing through Mexico on their way to America. We also need to stop the inflow of drugs from the cartels to the United States. Once we control those two issues we can work on a new trade agreement."

"Leal, what is happening with the "Stinging Hornet"?

"He is still a big problem. He is opposing my reform measures whenever he can."

"Please be careful. We both know he is very dangerous."

"I will. Harold, that advice applies to you too. The hornet has it in for you too as he considers you one of the reasons that Alto Roble is dead. He wants to even the score with you for negatively impacting his business and the flow of drugs through his cartel. He also blames you for losing a close friend, and a protective shield in the Mexican government."

"Thanks for the heads up about him. I know he hates me for several reasons. I want you to know that I have the same feelings for him. I consider him an evil man who has no heart, character, or soul. The world will be a better place when he no longer walks upon it."

"I agree Harold. He is human debris."

"When are you coming to America to go to a baseball game?"

"I want to come when you make your comeback."

"I want that to happen, and for you to be in the row by the dugout. I will make all of the arrangements for you and your family to be my guests. But, first I have to work hard and make my way back. I know what you mean about tough sledding. Making comebacks are hard work."

"I will look forward to that Harold. Is there anything I can do for you?"

"Just take me fishing if I get to Mexico again Leal."

"I will. Please come see us when you can."

"I accept you invitation. Please tell your wife and children hello. I am sending my prayers to all of you."

"Thank you my friend."

After hanging up the phone, Harold had reflected on his time in Mexico, the good fortune of finding Luisa again, and their time together. The flood of memories overwhelmed him, and he had felt a stream of tears come to his eyes. He had not gotten over losing Luisa, and had hoped that he would never lose his love for her.

After sitting in his chair by the window and looking at his loyal friends, the birds and the squirrels, for a few moments, he had gone to his bedroom and entered the large walk-in closet. He had taken a large box from the white metal racks above the clothes and had sat down on the bed. He had taken the contents out of the box and placed them next to him, on the bed.

    He had then waded through the pile of mementos from Luisa's and his time together in Mexico until he had come to a large manila-colored envelope. He had then removed the two eight-by-ten-inch pictures he wanted. One picture was of Luisa and the Servidor children at the playground where she had watched them as their nanny.

    The second picture was of Luisa and the Servidor family at the Mexico City airport on the day he and she had flown to America to start their new life together. He looked at the faces of the people in the picture. All were smiling broadly. Luisa had her arms around he children, who were also holding her hands.

    Gatewood had placed the picture and a personal note in the envelope, then had looked at Luisa's pictures for the last time before sealing the flap. With tears in his eyes, he had said, "Yes, she was very special. I loved her."

    Harold reflected on his thoughts about Leal Servidor and said, "Mexico is very lucky. They have a man of high character in office. And, America is lucky to have such a good friend in the Mexican presidency. He is a man who will follow through with his promises."

Chapter 3

Ready To Sting

February 19

THE STINGING HORNET, THE EL AVISPON PICANTE, was ready to strike. Things had not been going well for Salvador Masas. His supply of cocaine from the TCPLM had decreased due to the increased stranglehold the American CIO had placed on shipments coming out of Venezuela and headed for the Dominican Republic.

The TCPLM's main efforts were being placed in the Dominican Republic, which had caused less attention to be given to the delivery system through Central America, Mexico, and America. Salvador Masas was losing money because he had less product to deliver to the street junkies in the Southwestern United States and Canada.

He had complained to the head of the TCPLM, Diego Ramirez, but his displeasure had fallen on deaf ears. Ramirez had mentioned that increased seizures of deliveries from the Dominican Republic had put that operation in a dire situation. He had asked Salvador to be patient. Unfortunately, the Stinging Hornet was not a patient man.

Masas ran the largest drug cartel in Mexico, which spanned the Northern Mexico from the Eastern boundary line of New Mexico to the ocean on the Western side of Baja California. He employed thousands of people in his cartel family. He had a multi-layered operation that believed in violence first and good manners second.

He had bodyguards, bullet-proof cars, top-of-the- line surveillance equipment, airplanes, all-terrain vehicles, narco-submarines to deliver his cocaine, cell phones and communications equipment, world-class computer technology systems, guns and armament of all kinds, and a network off safe houses all across Mexico and the rest of the world.

He had lived in Mexico, Argentina, Guatemala, Paraguay, Columbia, Spain, and Italy, running his operation from afar. He had friends in the AIO, the Durante crime family, the Columbian Carmelo and Mountain Growers cartels, the office of the leader of Venezuela, and until recently, in the oval office of the president of Mexico.

Masas lived a fast, globe-trotting lifestyle, and important friends who could help him escape the legal authorities worldwide. He was married with children but also had a stable of beautiful women who catered to his every need. He lived like a king, and was not used to getting less than one hundred percent of what he wanted, and demanded.

He also had a terrible temper and would lash out at anyone who did not do as he instructed. He had been informed by Diego Ramirez that one of the main reasons for the reduction in cocaine headed to his cartel was partially caused by the efforts of Harold Gatewood in the Dominican Republic.

Masas had hated Gatewood from the first time he had seen him on Mexican President Alto Roble's yacht in Cabo San Lucas. Their meeting had been brief but Masas had vowed to kill Gatewood. That feeling had intensified with Gatewood's actions in Mexico, the death of his friend Alto Roble, and the situation in the Dominican Republic.

He was mad, and he wanted to take his anger out on Gatewood. His thinking was not clear, and he longed for his early years before he had become the head of the cartel. He remembered those years with affection, and let his mind go back to that time.

He had worked hard to become the most-feared, most-powerful cartel leader in the world. He, Salvador Masas, known as El Avispon Picante, the "stinging hornet", had joined the cartel after suffering a poor childhood, always one step ahead of total poverty. He had shot through the ranks of the organization due to his intelligence, cunning, skill set, and a total enjoyment of his personal version of ruthless killing.

He had killed unabatedly at all levels of the cartel. Rival cartel members, military personnel, police officers, politicians, tourists, and all levels of citizens were all victims of his bloodlust and desire to become a capo of the cartel. He had become a "made man" in the cartel when he killed a drug pusher who had refused to pony up the cartel's share of the transactions. He had killed his mentor when it became evident that he could seize control of the cartel, located in Northern Mexico.

Salvador had eliminated rival capos when it suited his goal for consolidating power, with himself in control. One-by-one, he had sent friends and enemies to the graveyard in his quest to be the head of all the cartels in Mexico. He remained in power by continuing his vise-like grip on the drug trade, working with the politicians, military, and police at all levels, and using an approach that "when cash will not buy you what you need, bullets and murder will".

He was feared by all people in the country, and had become a massive problem for all of the law enforcement agencies in the world. He was on America's ten most wanted list, ranking number one. He was Fermin Zuzen and the Agence de Renseignement's most popular, desired target, also being number one on their list of criminals.

His operation had enjoyed a good working relationship as a smuggler of drugs for the Columbian and Venezuelan cartels and the TCPLM, and had grown as a the preeminent drug trafficking cartel when the United States began cooperating with the above mentioned governments to crack down on the cartels. His business savvy and ruthlessness allowed him to seize the opportunity, and become the most successful, powerful drug cartel in the world.

He developed distribution channels into America. His production facilities and an organization that ran as smooth as a fine, Swiss watch allowed him to become one of the richest people in the world. His organizational members loved him. They also feared him, as they knew they were only one disloyal act away from meeting their maker if they stepped out of line. He demanded, and received, total respect and control of the operation from the tinniest detail to the most sophisticated operational plan. He was master of his domain.

He changed his location each day, sleeping in different homes and safe houses throughout Mexico and other countries, and had avoided numerous attempts by the United States and the Agence de Renseignement to capture, arrest, and extradite him to face prosecution and jail time. He had the resources to pay off the politicians, and to prevent extradition if captured, to support his upscale lifestyle, and to maintain his freedom. His inner circle consisted of intelligent, loyal employees and a well-trained, and heavily-armed, band of soldiers willing to die to protect him.

Masas had socialized freely with Alto Roble, the president of Mexico, and Ramon Nazoa, the president of Venezuela. All three of them shared a total hatred of a common enemy, the United States. Both presidents had hated America for its constant interference in the internal affairs in their country.

Salvador Masas hated America for its efforts to disrupt his cartel's business. He felt that they had no right to interfere with his drug smuggling. After all, if the American populace wanted to buy drugs, he was only filling a void in the market. If he were put out of business that void would be filled by another supplier. He could not comprehend the fact that America could be so naïve.

Masas' operation had suffered setbacks before. The TCPLM employee in charge of scheduling deliveries to the Dominican Republic and to Mexico had provided information to the CIO as a favor to Harold Gatewood, who had been operating in Mexico. That employee was his lover, Lucia Gaicia.

He had been pleased to learn of the death of Luisa Gaicia. She had fled with her lover, Harold Gatewood, to Gibson City, Illinois. She had met a gruesome experience of torture and death. He did not know who Susana Richards, the killer, was or that she even existed. But, he was thankful she had killed Luisa, as it had saved him the trouble of doing so.

He could not have ever forgiven Luisa for the lost profits, and business worries she had caused his cartel. But, forgiveness was not his long suit anyway. In his entire life the stinging hornet had never forgiven anyone who had caused him pain, as such an action was not in his DNA.

Also on the list of people who were causing him trouble and making his disposition unpleasant was the new president of Mexico, Leal Servidor. Masas hated him simply because he had replaced his friend and fellow carouser Sergio Rojas. That action was more than enough for Masas' hatred, and desire to kill Servidor. The hatred grew and became more intense as Masas viewed him as an imposter in the office.

Servidor's political plans and objectives were dangerous obstacles to the cartel's flow of profits, and the hornet's personal lifestyle. Masas had decided that Servidor would be killed. Only the time had yet to be decided.

Masas had one other person on his list to quickly exterminate, the man he hated most, Harold Gatewood. He held the ballplayer responsible for all of the cartel's problems. If Gatewood had not gone to Venezuela he would not have met and swept Luisa off her feet. She had fallen totally in love with him from the first time she had met him, and accidently thrown her salad on him at the restaurant.

Gatewood's charm had bowled Luisa over and she was in his power immediately. If they had never met she would have stayed at the TCPLM, and would have never given Gatewood the information on the delivery schedules and routes into Mexico and he Dominican Republic.

If she would have never met Gatewood she would have never been held captive, forced to leave Venezuela, and end up as the nanny for the Leal Servidor family in Mexico. She would never have been reunited with Gatewood if he had not gone to Mexico City to scout for baseball players.

Yes, Harold Gatewood was the impetus who set off the chain of events that had led to Sergio Roble's death, Leal Servidor's ascent to the presidency, and the beginning of the problems for the hornet and the cartel.

Truthfully, Masas had hated Gatewood since he had first seen him on Roble's yacht when they were in Cabo San Lucas. He had despised Gatewood's squeaky clean image, his gentlemanly manner that drew beautiful women to him from all over the world, his high character, his sense of humor, and his ability to have kings, presidents, and all classes of people like him.

Masas also knew that Gatewood was everything he was not. People only pretended to like Masas, and he knew it. He also knew that due to his looks, lack of personality and manners, and the fact that he was completely devoid of a sense of humor, he would never be Gatewood's equal, even though he ran one of the largest, most powerful cartels in the world. Gatewood was just a ballplayer, and a washed-up one at that.

He held Gatewood responsible for the cartel's losses. Drug shipments had declined forty-five percent, and Masas felt as though he was losing his control of his cartel. He had cobbled together efforts that had increased the cartels earnings in the human trafficking, kidnapping, and extortion areas.

The cartel had also been paid handsomely for helping the United Syrian Freedom fighters, the USFF, establish training camps near the American border. Despite these successes in replacing lost income, Masas felt like a failure, and he blamed Gatewood. There was only one solution to his paranoia.

He must kill Gatewood. He could have one of his sicarios, a hitman, do it, but he wanted to do it himself. He envisioned wrapping his hands around Gatewood's throat and choking the life out of him. He would enjoy watching Gatewood struggle for his breath, turn purple, and then slump lifelessly into death. Yes, Masas knew that killing Gatewood would solve all of his problems.

At least, that is what his revenge-fueled, twisted state of mind grasped as reality.

Chapter 4

There Was Plenty To Go Around

February 20

THERE WAS PLENTY OF HATRED FOR HAROLD GATEWOOD TO GO AROUND. The people of Venezuela were restless. The knowledge of TCPLM leader Sergio Rojas' death, and his fall from the cable car high above the city, would have made headlines in the newspapers if these were normal times. But, times were far from normal. Each day, the people were becoming more dissatisfied with conditions in the Caracas, and in the country. President Nazoa's government was starting to unravel, and he needed to install calm before it as too late.

    He stood at his office window that faced the courtyard below, the same as he had done four days ago. He remembered his thoughts of March sixth. His favorite companions, the birds, were still chirping and enjoying their lives. Nazoa again wanted to be a bird so he could fly far away, to a place where he could be happy. Conditions in the country had reached a tipping point. If he were forced from office he would try to go to a country that would give him asylum.

    The Nazis had lived in Argentina and Brazil after escaping. He had stolen more money from the country than a person could possibly spend in a lifetime. He would use that money to buy his freedom. He mused at the thought that he had once relished his rise to power and the perceived glory it would provide. It had turned out to be a series of nightmarish events that were all coming to a close in the probable final chapter of his reign. He hoped to escape with his head still intact, and his stash of wealth waiting for him.

    He needed to try to hold his government together in hope of a miracle occurring. Perhaps the price of oil would leap forward, allowing income to pour into the country as it once had. He had been trying to convince the Middle East countries to curtail production, create a shortage in the world market, drive up the price, stabilize the now depressed market, and once again place the oil producing countries in a wealthy position. He could salvage the country, and his position as its leader, if he could deliver on that miracle.

    Much to his dismay, the Middle Eastern oil-producing countries had suffered an overriding problem that had stopped the cooperative market manipulation attempt in its tracks, the Arab independence movement. He had always hated the American government for their interference in world economics.

He especially hated the current American president, and Nazoa was relishing the end of the American leader's two terms in office. He had equal hatred for the feckless Secretary of State who had pushed for removal of his fellow dictators whose iron-fisted control like his own had kept a lid on the populace in the Middle East. The two American leaders had kicked over the one domino that held the complicated balance of power in the region in check, without planning on how to stop the tide of problems that would fall in the Middle East as a result of their mistake.

Now, constant streams of immigrants were fleeing the region, heading to Europe, Central America, Mexico, and into America at record-breaking paces in hopes for a new life. Some immigrants had other goals, and carried plans of terrorism against the regions they were invading. It was now an increasingly-dangerous world. Countries were buckling at the waves of people illegally invading their countries.

At least Nazoa did not face an immigrant problem, as no one wanted to come to Venezuela. Everyone wanted to leave the country, due to current conditions. His socialist government had failed. Events were returning to near-barbaric levels. People had shortages of food, and were eating dogs, cats, and pigeons. Grocery stores had shortages, and delivery trucks of supplies were being attacked by the people in the streets. Armed military units were being used to guard the delivery trucks. Many people were going hungry, and were raiding the garbage cans in the city to find food.

Shortages existed in food, medicine, and household goods such as toilet paper. Rationing and long waiting lines were the norm. To fight the problem, Nazoa had ordered able-bodied people to work in the fields for two to four months. A lack of clean water to drink was causing people to become sick, and there was no medicine to make them well. Electricity was in short supply. And, despite its cheap price, power outages were the norm.

Inflation was running wild, up almost two thousand percent in the last four years. The economy was reeling, shrinking almost twenty percent in the last three years. Government price controls had failed as there was no incentive for manufactures to produce anything. The country was now importing everything. Despite being one of the world's biggest oil producing countries, Venezuela was buying oil from its hated enemy, the United States. The nationally-run oil company's revenue was down so far that it could not pay its mounting debts.

Socialism had run its course, and like other such experiments in the world in Russia and Cuba, it needed a shot of capitalism to make a rebound. Nazoa hoped to escape before the house of cards came tumbling down, taking him with it. He closed his eyes and imagined he was flying high above the ground, looking for a safe place to land, and build a new nest.

But, before Nazoa would make flight to his new location he had one item he wanted to complete, the killing of Harold Gatewood for all of the misery he had caused him.

Chapter 5

"This time my friends"

February 22

DIEGO RAMIREZ SAT IN THE OUTER OFFICE OF the TCPLM building looking at the empty desk that was formerly the workspace of Luisa Gaicia. He could not help himself. Tears came to his eyes as he remembered Luisa. She had always been kind to him, and he had always returned the favor. She was a jewel, one which the likes of her he would never find again.

Ramirez had come to power due to the death of Sergio Rojas. Rojas had been shot and killed by Harold Gatewood when the former head of the TCPLM refused to jump to his death from the top of the cable car in the mountains outside Caracas.

Ramirez had been with Rojas and the TCPLM since he joined the organization as a teenager. Rojas had invaded his village and rained havoc on the people due to his need to instill their total cooperation in the drug business. Rojas was a survivor and had joined the TCPLM to escape his dismal surroundings and to live what he perceived to be an exciting lifestyle as a cartel member.

He had moved up through the ranks in the organization and was chosen to be Sergio's right-hand man due to his intelligence, and loyalty. He had supported Rojas at every step along the way, despite his disdain for the brutal tactics that had made him rich and powerful. In truth, he despised Rojas for his inhuman actions, and in particular, for his treatment of Luisa Gaicia.

Ramirez had been smitten with her since Rojas kidnapped her from the small, poor village in Columbia. She was a teenager when Rojas moved her into his home and made her his sex slave and his lover.

He had beaten her repeatedly and had forced her to have an abortion when she had become pregnant.

He had brought her to Caracas when he opened a new office there. She worked for him in the office handling the scheduling and distribution routes of the supply lines of cocaine from Columbia through Venezuela to the Dominican Republic.

The TCPLM was in partnership with the Venezuelan government. The whole country was involved in drogas, drugs. The military, the cartel drug dealers, called the traficante de drogas, were all in business together. It was a totally corrupt association. Luisa was an efficient worker in the TCPLM and was in the center of the operation due to her job duties and her association, awful as it was for her, with Rojas.

Ramirez had been in love with her from the first time he had seen her and hated Rojas for his treatment of her. Diego was possessed by the idea of being with her.

As he looked at her empty desk he thought of an incident where Rojas had belittled her in the office. He remembered it verbatim as it had related to Luisa spending time with the American baseball player Harold Gatewood, a man Ramirez truly hated.

Rojas had summoned Luisa into his office and immediately, a shouting match had burst forth. Ramirez mentally replayed the entire conversation.

Rojas had been the first to speak. "Luisa, I know what you are up to. You will never again see that man."

She had answered, "I will see him whenever I want Sergio."

"No, I will not allow that."

"I have a life. I intend to live it as I see fit."

"You belong to me."

"I don't belong to anyone."

"You are mine."

"No, you want to control me."

"I forbid you to see him."

"I will see him."

"I told you I would kill your family if you ever tried to leave me."

"You will not do that."

"Why not?"

"Because if you do that it that would cause me to hate you more than I do now."

"I swear I will kill them."

"Then I will leave."

"I will never let you do that. You will stay here."

"You have many women."

"I still own you."

"I am not a trophy or a bird you can keep in a cage."

"You know I can be very dangerous."

"You have beaten me and raped me for years. That is why I hate you."

"I will rape you again."

"Then I will hate you even more."

"I will beat you with my belt."

"It will do you no good. I would rather be dead than be with you."

"A good beating has always made you see the light."

"It is useless Sergio. I do not care to live if you continue to force me to stay."

"You have no place to go."

"I will find a place. I will be happy anywhere as long as I am away from you."

"It is the American, the ballplayer, Harold Gatewood, isn't it?"

"Yes. He is wonderful. But, I decided to leave you years ago. I need to get out of this prison in which you have me confined."

"I saw you eating lunch with him every day last week."

"Yes. It was fantastic to be with him."

"I watched you go dancing."

"Yes, it was great fun."

"And, you went to the movies with him."

"Of course, I want to be with him every minute of the day."

"I saw you go to his hotel. I know you stayed with him until the next morning."

"Yes I did. We made love many times. He is kind, and the best lover I have had in my whole life."

"I made love to you."

"No, you forced me to have sex with you. There is a big difference."

"I am a great lover."

"No, you are a disgusting pig. You don't measure up to him in any way."

"I can kill him."

"That would only make me want to kill you."

"I forbid you to see him again."

"Stay away from me Sergio. I will do what I want. And, I will be with him whenever I want."

After her final comment of rebellion, with tears streaming down her face, Luisa walked to the women's lounge to compose herself. Ramirez had said to her, "I am sorry you had to go through that. I feel sorry for you Luisa. Sergio has treated you like dirt for years."

Ramirez shook his head as he remembered what had happened after the incident. She had spent the night with Gatewood. In the morning she had returned to her apartment to get ready for work. Sergio Rojas had shown up unannounced and proceeded to beat her unmercifully. She had arrived at the office wearing sunglasses to cover her blacken eyes, and a sweater to cover the bruises on her arms.

Ramirez had vowed that he would always treat her nicely if she would move in with him. He loved her with all of her heart. As much as he hated Gatewood for what had transpired after he killed Sergio Rojas, Ramirez was glad his employer had met his maker.

After Rojas's death, Ramirez had rescued Luisa from the farm where the monster had beaten and nearly killed her. Diego had taken her to the clinic near the TCPLM training camp in the mountains and had returned to bring her back to Caracas once she had recovered. He had found out that she had left to make her way to America to be with Gatewood.

Ramirez had killed the doctor who had released her. After being given false information by the doctor, he had set out to find her, but had initially been sent in the wrong direction. Once his path had been corrected he had always been one step behind her on her journey through Columbia, Panama, Belize, Costa Rica, and Mexico. She had proceeded on to America with Gatewood, where she met her death.

His hatred for Gatewood had developed into an out- of-control obsession. Someday, he would find the ballplayer and kill him.

Ramirez's thoughts returned to the purpose of the meeting today. He was to discuss the interruption of the supply lines through the Dominican Republic for the drug cartels. Two leaders of the Columbian drug cartels and one crime family head in Venezuela would be guests at the meeting.

Diego Ramirez proceeded to review his assessments of each leader, starting with Lino Pascual, perceived head of the Montanas las Productores, the Mountain Producers cartel. Contacts with the cartel were made with Pascual, but the real man behind the throne was unknown. Whoever he was, he had managed to keep his identity secret.

Lino had ascended to be the front man of the cartel when his brother Ruben was arrested, extradited to America by the Columbian government, and convicted on charges under the racketeering influenced and corruption organizations program, the RICO act. The RICO law allowed America to bring leaders of foreign criminal organizations to trail. Ruben was still in jail and was expected to maintain that address for many years.

The Mountain Producers cartel was still the strongest drug producing organization in Columbia despite Ruben's conviction, and the unknown factor of Lino's desire to wrestle control of the cartel from the true man behind the scenes, Mateo Amon. Also unknown was the hatred Amon had for Gatewood as his daughter Sofia had died when she was hiking with Gatewood in Ella Se Cayo, Venezuela.

One of the Mountain Producer's biggest strengths was the fact that they operated in the mountains, in the think jungle, and enjoyed the support of the locals, many of whom were still being paid by the cartel to grow cocaine. They were a guerilla organization with deep ties to the area.

The Columbian military had not been able to dent their organization. Their network used producers who were loyal, and felt a kinship with the organization. The cartel members lived like animals in the jungle. They were a tough bunch, a true adversary of the Columbian government.

Ramirez also thought that they were a very good customer and that they would be receptive to his suggestions, as they used the TCPLM as their first choice for marketing their cocaine.

The second Columbia cartel at the meeting would be the Carmelo cartel, headed by Rafael Carmelo, the Hombre del Carmelo. His nickname meant the "candy man." He heads the crime family that has paid the TCPLM handsomely to bribe our military and politicians here in Venezuela for our distribution systems. He is also a good customer.

We are still using some of the older distribution routes to move some of his product. We are still moving cocaine from Columbia to here, then to Central America, then Mexico, and finally into the United States.

Carmelo has friends in the Central American and Mexican governments that work with him. He also pays large bribes to the United States border agents to allow shipments to cross into the Southwestern states. He knows which agents can be corrupted.

Ramirez knew the American border patrol had many good people who had their hands tied by the American president but Carmelo could get to the bad apples and move his product across their border.

Ramirez knew that it was a pity that the American politicians had not enforced their borders. Their inaction had resulted in a business boom for the TCPLM. The last eight years had been open season for drugs, and terrorists, to move into the United States.

We could not have placed a more beneficial person for us in their White House as they did when they elected the feckless one many years ago. The whole world was laughing at him. But, Ramirez knew he should not look negatively at such a wonderful, unexpected gift that had been dropped into their lap.

Ramirez was aware that the original distribution route through Central America and Mexico into the United States was somewhat secure in its operation at the present time. The real problem to be discussed in the meeting today was the stability of the Venezuelan government and their reduced capacity to protect the distribution system from the country to the Caribbean countries of Cuba, Hatti, and the Dominican Republic, and the United States territory of Puerto Rico.

The cooperation of the Bertalina government in Cuba had been lessened since the failure of the attempted coup by now-deceased General Domingo.

Ramirez hoped that he could entice Cuba to come back into the fold. He was well aware that Bertalina's friendship with the American baseball player Harold

Gatewood had complicated Cuba's business relationship with the TCPLM. He viewed it as another good reason to kill Gatewood.

The last member to be in attendance at the meeting was the head of the largest crime family in Venezuela, Fabbri Durante. He was the member most impacted by the interruption of the supply lines to the Dominican Republic. Durante had close ties with his fellow Sicilian crime families and supplied most of the drugs that went to Europe. Spain, France, England, Belgium, and the rest of Europe were dependent on the Durante family to deliver cocaine for street usage. His shipments to America were also being curtailed.

The Durante crime family was losing vast amounts of money every day due to the interruption of deliveries, and Ramirez expected Fabbri Durante to be the most upset of his three guests.

Ramirez's thoughts were interrupted by news that all three of his guests were present. He welcomed each man as they arrived. Pascual, Carmelo, and Durante were ushered into the meeting room. The conversation started cordially as each man took a seat.

Rafael Carmelo, sat motionless in front of the Ramirez. He was a handsome man, with movie star looks, and an air of confidence that bordered on conceit. He was immaculately dressed, and wore enough gold jewelry to pass for an Olympic athlete who had won five gold medals.

He was a ladies man, with a girl in every port. He eyed everyone in the room with caution and was uncomfortable being in Caracas with his cocaine rivals. He had agreed to the TCPLM's previous distribution and protection terms but he had always followed a success plan that was founded on the principle of trusting no one and remaining cautious.

Lino Pascual was seated on Ramirez's right, next to Diaz and Emilo. While Pascual was not the true head of the Mountain Producers cartel he played the part well. He was dressed conservatively, like a businessman, in a beige-colored suit, beige shirt, brown tie with white dots, brown socks, and a pair of highly-shined brown slip-on shoes.

He was of how a typical Columbian looked in terms of his skin and hair color, facial hair, dark eyes, and straight, white teeth. He too was suspicious of the purpose of the meeting and was looking forward to hearing the details of the program.

Fabbri Durante was seated on Ramirez's left. He was nervous, and shifted his body continuously in his seated position, as if his pants were sticking to the chair's seat, and that his movement would give him freedom. He could have played a part in a Hollywood mafia movie, as he had the look of a gangster.

His olive skin, dark eyes, heavy eyebrows, and stocky build were stereotypical Italian. He was bald, with long hair on the sides head pulled back into a small ponytail at the back of his head. His persona was that of a mean man, and it was accurate.

Ramirez continued, "My friends, we are here today to talk about the status of the interruption of our cocaine trafficking business to the Dominican Republic and through Mexico. Several factors are impacting our efforts. As you can see, the representatives of the Nazoa government are not present as their stability will be a topic of our meeting, which will be confidential."

All three members reported that they had spoken with President Nazoa about the problems in his government and were brought up to date about his actions to improve the situation in the county.

"I am glad that you have talked to the president. We all want him to remain in office to stabilize our business relationship, which has been positive and cooperative over the years. We all have an understanding with Nazoa. We pay him to keep the military on our good side, and to assist our shipments of drugs to our locations outside of the country."

"It has been a good association. I asked you here today to discuss how we can make that situation permanent and to assure you that we have made improvements in our services for you, our customers, and partners."

All three guests voiced concerns over the recent disclosure of the distribution routes and receiving points in receiving countries that operated as a shipping base to America and Europe.

"Gentlemen, our mole, Ms. Luisa Gaicia, who worked in our office, and forwarded the operational details to Harold Gatewood and the CIO, has been killed in America. The internal problem that was one of the causes of the recent interrupted supply deliveries has been corrected. I have reworked our delivery routes to countries outside Venezuela, and have had our receiving bases moved to different locations. We have solved that problem."

The news was met with open arms, relief, and also a warning that all three of the guests would not tolerate another such incident. They lost vast amounts of money during the disruption period. They wanted assurance that no other disloyal employees could cause such a similar occurrence again.

"You have that assurance from me. Any employee who acts in such a manner will be instantly killed. Also, I have initiated a backup system of checks and balances in our system that did not exist before. My predecessor, Sergio Rojas, was romantically involved with Ms. Gaicia, and did not check on her work or her loyalty. That will not happen with me in charge."

The three guests seemed to agree with Ramirez's guarantee. They wanted to know what Nazoa had told him in order to make sure each of them were being told the same story.

"Nazoa also told me that he has staved off a public recall that would certainly led to his removal from office. He also stated he has shored up his political base and is in no danger of impeachment. He is arresting and disposing off his political opponents and has control of his political destiny."

All three asked about the state of the country's economy.

"I was assured that the public is now somewhat reassured that better times are ahead. He has raised the minimum wage six times this year to appease the public's fear of runaway inflation. Most encouraging was his statement that the Middle East Oil Carte Countries Organization, MEOCCO, has agreed to limit production, starting with a twenty-five percent reduction in drilling. The reduced supply will help raise the price of oil and bring money into the national treasury."

All three guests wanted to know about the other internal supply problems of food and medicine.

"The military is handling the distribution of food and medicine. Apart from some good, old-fashioned, black-marketing action by the military, that problem appears to be under control. And, after all gentlemen, we would also engage in a little black-marketing if we were in their shoes."

Pascual, Carmelo, and Durante all wanted to know about the mass immigration from the country to Columbia, Brazil, the Central Americas, Europe, and America.

"I was assured that even though it looks bad, it is a good thing, as the most disgruntled people are leaving. The result is a remaining population is one that can more easily controlled with iron-fisted tactics if need be."

All three men wanted to know how their shipments could continue if Nazoa was forced from power.

"Then we will reinstitute the Venezuelan way, the way of corruption, which characterizes the country. We bought Nazoa and we will buy the next person in charge if we need to."

All agreed that that option sounded reasonable but wanted to know what path they should plan as a backup option if a do-gooder like Leal Servidor in Mexico took power.

"We need to plan for that contingency. But, accidents do happen, even to do-gooder presidents. A person such as that will have to fight the inbred corruption of the Venezuelan political and economic systems. We can outlast such a person if one would become president."

Fabbri Durante spoke up with a concern. "As we all know, I have been most impacted by the supply line interruption to the Dominican Republic because most all of my drug supply goes to Europe. I will not allow my operation to be compromised due to outside interference. I will take matters into my own hands and eliminate anyone who stands in my way."

"How would you plan to do that Fabbri?"

"Obviously, my Sicilian contacts would send someone talented in the art of trash removal to correct the situation. Our first soldier, Baldovino Gioele, was called Il Barbiere, The Barber. Unfortunately, he was killed in Gatewood's room before he could eliminate the ballplayer. He did kill Gatewood's girlfriend before he was shot. I have another soldier in mind who will get the job done this time my friends."

Pascual, Carmelo, and Ramirez all gave the green light to Durante to take whatever action needed to protect his interests, as they would all do the same if they were in his position. They all also pledged to help if needed.

They meeting ended on a positive note in terms of approaching the reinstitution of the supply lines. As the meeting was about to break up, Durante said he had one more item to bring up for discussion. "I have noticed that one man's name continues to come up in our discussion of what and who has caused us problems. It is always America that sticks their nose into our business, and the name of a seemingly unassuming baseball player, Harold Gatewood, pops up. I want all of you to know that I will not bow to either. I will kill him if he interferes with us again."

Diego Ramirez turned his head away from his guests so that they would not see the smile on his face. He snickered and said, "If I can't kill Gatewood myself then maybe Durante's Sicilian buddies can do it for me."

Chapter 6

"For Sofia"

February 23

LINO PASCUAL, THE PERCIEVED HEAD OF THE MOUNTAIN PRODUCERS CARTEL, spoke to his right-hand man, Alfonso Roderigo, about his plans for the day.
"Alfonso, I mentioned the other day that I am going to Ella Se Cayo to meet with Mateo Amon."
"Yes, I remember."
"I will be back late tonight, or by noon tomorrow, depending on Mateo's plans for me. If we have to shoot pool and then tour the banana production facilities it may be tomorrow. I will try to get out of there as soon as I can."
"I will make sure everything in the operation runs smoothly."
"I know I am leaving things in your capable hands Alfonso."
Lino entered his vehicle, turned on the cd player and started to listen to the folk rhythm beat of the music style native to the plains of Columbia and Venezuela, the joropo. Lino sang and bobbed his head to the beat of the fandango-type music, which combined African, native Columbian and Venezuelan, and European influences. It was creole music, and suited Lino's tastes perfectly.
Many thoughts ran through Pascual's head as he drove the winding, narrow roads down the mountains to the valley below. He had brought increased production and bottom-line income to the cartel operation. While he had been compensated handsomely, he did not feel he was appreciated. He had made decisions that had brought millions of extra profits to the organization.
What really bothered him was Mateo Amon's lack of recognition for his efforts. This factor, combined with a desire to head the cartel himself had fueled his disappointment, then anger with Mateo.
He knew he could run the operation better than his employer. His lack of respect for Mateo had festered, n and grown into total disrespect and disdain. He was ready to oust Mateo and be the true head of the cartel. He had crafted

a plan of deceit, murder, and takeover, and he was poised to implement the daring coup.

Lino did not believe that Mateo was aware of his plan, as it had been kept secret. He considered Mateo a weak man, unaware that without him, the cartel would wither away and die, or be taken over by a stronger band of drug producers. The time was near for Mateo to voluntary step down, or forcibly be removed from power. Lino had also planned for another option, one that would separate Mateo from his earthly presence.

As he proceeded along the roads that led to Ella Se Cayo, Lino recalled his thoughts of the last time he had been summoned to Mateo's home to discuss the attack on the warehouse that destroyed millions of dollars of cocaine supply.

He closed his eyes for an instant as the thoughts overtook his concentration. He spoke to himself, "I remember that when I gave Mateo the news about the attack on the facility, and the very being of the cartel, it was met with a calm, measured reaction by the head of the organization. I knew that Mateo would then place a plan into action that would determine who was responsible, where the guilty parties could be located, and a timetable for retribution."

Lino continued his recollection of the event, "I had said that I would not want to be the responsible parties for the attack, as their death would be carried out in a particularly brutal fashion. Attacking the cartel was not good for a person's health, and soon dead bodies would be turning up. The cartel's message would be clear, do not mess with us or you will pay in a horrific way."

Despite his disdain for Mateo Amon, he was still a dangerous man when he mustered up the energy to be so.

As he approached Ella Se Cayo, a city on the Venezuelan border with Columbia, Lino knew the routine he would face when he reached Amon estate. He would walk to the front door, be met by the butler, and ushered to a sitting room to wait for Mateo. He dreaded what would then once again follow.

Mateo Amon would welcome him, they would sit and visit for a short time in the sitting room, then Mateo would take him a nearby room to play pool, a game in which Lino did not excel, and hated. After some discussion on the state of the cartel and the discussion of any recent problems, Mateo would show Lino his banana operation. He would be required to visit the growing areas, and the factory. The tour would be torture for him, as his host would be very talkative about the business he loved so much. He was wild about the banana business, a condition that Lino considered borderline psychotic.

During the tour Lino would hear the story about the Amon family's big party for many of the local dignitaries every year. It is a costume party. Mateo would describe how he always dressed as a banana. He would always say how his costume would cause so much embarrassment for his wife. But, after all of these years, he knew not to try to change the conversation when it came time for Mateo to discuss his love of the banana business.

Pascual turned off his vehicle engine and walked to the front door. He was met the butler who, as expected, led him to a sitting room to wait for his employer. His wait was a short one, as Mateo Amon, and his wife, greeted him.

As they shook hands, Pascual thought about the Amon's background.

Both were from a small town in Columbia, ten miles from the Venezuelan border. Lino did not know why, but that fact had stuck in his memory. The couple had married young, and moved to Venezuela when Mateo Amon had started law school in Ella Se Cayo. After law school he started his law practice in the town, quickly invested in banana farms, then moved into the banana processing business. The Amon efforts were an outstanding example of people's ability to start from nothing and build success upon success.

Mateo Amon was an educated and successful man, a lawyer and a businessman, cultured, refined, and gentlemanly. He had been a ruggedly handsome man, and had enjoyed an air of confidence. Pascual was shocked to see how Mateo had aged since his last visit.

His hair, eyebrows, and mustache were now gray, no doubt from the stress of their daughter Sofia's death while hiking with her lover Harold Gatewood, the American baseball player who had become a persistent thorn in the side of all of the cartels in Columbia.

Mrs. Amon had been a pretty and outgoing woman. She also was educated, successful, cultured, and very loving. She was an artist, and had always been dressed in a white painter's smock, adorned with many paint smudges in the bright blue, red, white, gold, and green colors she used in her craft, when they had previously met.

She also had aged, as her hair had turned white. She had lost weight and looked skeleton-thin, and her radiant smile had transformed into downturned wrinkles near the corners of her mouth. She was suffering from the same malady as her husband, the grief of losing their daughter Sofia.

Grief was not first-time visitor to the Amon family. They had lost four unborn children due to miscarriages, prior to Sofia's birth. She was a gift from heaven and had been spoiled since birth. When Lino mentioned that he was hopeful the couple was making progress adjusting to the loss of Sofia, Mrs. Amon's facial expression changed, as she beamed with pride at the mention of her daughter's name.

The Amon's were one of the richest, most successful, well-respected families in Venezuela, but like all families, they could not escape God's plan. Unfortunately, Sofia's death was part of the Amon story, and the couple was learning to live with the tragedy. Despite what Lino had planned for Mateo he did feel sorry for the couple's loss.

After Mrs. Amon excused herself in order to continue her painting, the men sat down in the chairs in the sitting room and started to speak.

"Thank you for coming here today Lino."

"I am always at your service Sir."

"I always appreciate your excellent work Lino."

"Thank you Sir."

"Before we talk about the cartel business I want to ask you if you are happy with your position at the cartel."

"Yes Sir, I am. You have been very gracious and supportive of my efforts. I appreciate that very much."

"Good. You know that I expect, and reward, loyalty."

"Yes Sir. You know I am loyal."

"I do. You have run the cartel in an excellent manner."

"Thank you."

"I hope you are enjoying your life and are able to do what pleases you when you are not at the production facility or the headquarters in the mountains."

"I am Sir. I thank you for letting me have enough vacation to get away."

"How is Alfonso Roderigo performing in your absence?"

"He is doing well. He knows the business and is aware of what you expect of me. In turn, he knows what I expect of him in order to make sure the cartel succeeds."

"Very good work. You have done a good job of mentoring his progress."

"Thank you Sir."

"Lino, I want to talk to you about the supply problems, the shipments into the Dominican Republic, and the problems in the Venezuelan government. Let's shoot some pool while we discuss those matters."

"Yes Sir, I would enjoy that."

As the two men headed to the pool room, Lino Pascual said to himself, "I was hoping to avoid this torture. Oh how I hate to play pool."

As the men chalked up their pool cues, Mateo Amon spoke, "Please tell me about the supply problem."

"The distribution supply routes were compromised when a worker in the Caracas office of the TCPLM gave the information to her lover, Harold Gatewood, who then gave the specific details to the CIO. As such, they knew when and where our shipments were to be made in the routes through Central

America to Mexico to the Southwestern United States, and the flights into the Dominican Republic."

"Did you say Harold Gatewood?"

"Yes. I am sorry to have to mention his name Sir, as I know he was responsible for your daughter Sofia's death. I must apologize as I know that information causes you grief."

"Do not worry about it. I need to know that and I am glad you told me."

"Thank you Sir."

"What is the status of the Venezuelan national government?"

"The country is in shambles. The oil price has started to go up as the oil producing countries in the Middle East have agreed to cut production, which will cause a shortage and drive prices back up."

"Good."

"The citizens are in panic. There are shortages in food and medicine. The military is profiting by selling these two items on the black market. And, many people are fleeing the country to find food, medicine, jobs, and hope for the future."

"What about President Nazoa?"

"He has survived a recall election attempt and will probably not be impeached. He will stay in office, but no one knows for how long. He has raised the minimum wage six times to help the people fight inflation."

"What is the outlook?"

"It looks bleak for him, and for the country. There are so many problems."

"What plans have you started to bribe and control his possible successor?"

"Our contacts inside the government have identified the two people who might succeed Nazoa. We are building a file, and checking on their vices to see if we can control him through blackmail."

"Please send me that information."

"I will."

"What are you doing in the Caribbean?"

"We are back in business and the TCPLM has set up new delivery routes and drop points inside the country."

"Are we distributing the necessary bribe money to the Dominican Republic president and politicians?"

"Yes Sir. We are currently paying him within the budgeted payment range."

"Good work."

"How soon before we are back to our one hundred percent figure for total shipments?"

"We are currently at seventy-five percent. We should be at the one hundred percent in another month."

"Are they any obstacles that will delay that effort?"

"Not at this time."

"Do you think there is a scenario that might develop into a problem for our deliveries and cash flows?"

"As usual, it would come from the Americans if there is to be one."

"Are there any CIO agents operating in the Dominican Republic now?"

"None that are known of Sir."

"Very well Lino. Please monitor the American CIO presence in the Dominican Republic and let me know of any possible changes."

"I will Sir."

"Lino you need to work on your pool game."

"I am not in your league."

"Practice is the key."

Thankfully, Lino thought the pool torture had ended.

"Lino, we are now going to tour the banana plant. While we do I want to talk to you about Harold Gatewood."

Pascual's heart sank, as he was now going to be subjected to another banana plant tour. Mateo and Lino headed to the banana fields. Mateo conducted a seminar on the preference for deep, well-drained soil needed to grow a quality crop. He said that the climate in Columbia, where his banana crop was located, was ideal. He discussed his growth from a banana farmer to a banana processor and shipper. After touring the fields he shuttled Lino to his banana factory.

Mateo discussed the steps in the overall banana sales process. Fields used to grow bananas then needed to be harvested by picking the crop, and transporting it to the packing shed to hang and dry. At the next stage of the process larger bundles needed to be divided into more store-friendly bunches. The bananas next needed to be washed, dried, refrigerated, sorted by quality, labeled, shipped, and marketed world-wide.

Market research, machinery purchases and updates, and fertilizer management were also involved. Tractors, washing tanks, storage buildings, boxes, shipping docks, offices, and other equipment were needed. Mateo's company grew premium quality bananas that demanded a quality price.

He believed in taking good care of his employees with the best machinery, safety measures, and benefits in the industry. He was possessed by the banana business, and Lino, his mind now a conglomeration of mush, was glad to get back to the house so he could thank his employer and return to his vehicle for his escape from pool, the banana business, and start the ride back to the cartel headquarters in the mountains.

As he drove along the route home, he said to himself,

"He is even more frail, weak, grief-stricken, and senile than he was on my last visit. It is time for me to take him out and gain control of the cartel."

Mateo Amon had waved goodbye, walked to his office, dialed a number of a contractor he had heard about from his good friend and business associate, Damon Justice from America.

"Hello'"

"Hello. Can this call be traced?", asked Amon.

"No I use throw-away cell phones."

"My research tells me you perform a service I would like carried out."

"What kind of service?"

"Removal of an overly-ambitious employee."

"Is the package returnable or to be permanently removed?"

"Permanently removed."

"By what means?"

"Any, just so it is done."

"How many units are in the package?"

"One."

"The head of a country?"

"No."

"With nuts or without?"

"With."

"In what area of the world is this package located?"

"It is located in the mountains of Columbia."

"Would the disposal service need to be done in public?"

"No,"

"Is the package heavily guarded?"

"No but he is a dangerous man in his own right."

"Are you worried about collateral damage to other packages?"

"No."

"Payment for disposal fees are based on many factors. The location is remote Sir. The package would know his environment and I would not so the fee will be higher."

"I understand."

"One other thing, dangers encountered in disposal, my exit after disposal, and quick access to another location."

"Ok. Go on please."

"The more severe the dangers the higher the disposal fee. So the fee charged will also take those factors into consideration."

Amon answered, "Understood."

"When is the disposal date for the package?"

"As soon as possible."

"Is the disposal for an aware or unsuspecting package?"
"Unsuspecting."
"Have you contacted other package disposal firms?"
Amon proudly stated, "No. I only purchase services from the world's best vendors."
"Will you be near the package disposal location?"
"No."
"We guarantee total package disposal."
"Excellent."
"Disposal fees vary."
"I understand. What is the range?"
"It will cost one million dollars for total package disposal in a location such as mentioned."
"It seems a little high."
"Top of the line, world-class work demands an appropriate price."
"Alright"
"The disposal location must be known so disposal routes and times can be arranged."
"How much planning is involved in this type of package disposal?"
"Based on the location and escape risks of this disposal, six weeks from the delivery and receipt of the first half of the fee."
"What about last minute changes?"
"Small changes in the disposal are not a problem in either cost or service areas."
"How are payments for disposal handled?"
"You will send it by wire to a numbered account. You will pay half down and half upon disposal of the package."
"Did you ever have a client who did not pay your fees?"
"None that are alive now to tell about it", replied the assassin.
"I want the package disposal service."
"Do you have any questions?"
"Yes."
"Go ahead please."
"How long have you been in the disposal business?", asked Amon.
"Over thirty years."
"Is your service totally confidential?"
"Yes."
"That is a must for my needs. It must be adhered to at all times. Otherwise, I will not utilize your services."
"Of course, I understand. For both the client, and the firm, confidentiality is completely guaranteed."

"If events change and the package removal is not desired any more, then there is no charge?"

"The charge would be for any expenses incurred, and half of the total fee. No work would be done prior to entering into an agreement for disposal services of the package."

"Okay. I want the service performed. Where do I wire the first payment?"

After the discussion of the details of the payment transaction and other details related to the contract-for- hire killing, Mateo Amon said, "There is one more thing. I will want you to perform a second contract for me once this first one is completed."

"Do you know the details of that contract need?"

"Not at this time."

"Then we will conclude our first contract, and I will then be happy to work with you again on your second contractual need."

Mateo Amon remembered his thoughts about the phone call. He had thanked his new contract-for-hire assassin, and smiled. He had known he would then finally get to the man who was responsible for the death of his beautiful daughter Sophia. Harold Gatewood would soon get what was coming to him.

Mateo stood with a stern look on his face, gave the matter more thought, and said, "Justice will be done." He then looked out upon his estate and remembered the days of his daughter's childhood when she had played in the large yard in front of him. He smiled and said, "For Sofia."

Chapter 7

Operacion Para Romper

February 24

OLD SCORES ARE SOMETIMES HARD TO SETTLE. The AIO had still not settled their old score with Harold Gatewood. They still bore the shame they had endured by not eliminating their American nemesis, Harold Gatewood, and all of their membership was still demanding blood for the loss of their loyal agents who had been killed in the pursuit of Harold's head.

National Commander Ekain Koldo had grown old and discouraged by the failure to successfully remove Gatewood, and his gray hair and the deep, dark bags under his eyes caused by lack of sleep and worry verified his passage into his twilight years.

Koldo's driver sat behind the wheel of the black, four-door luxury car as it pulled into the right lane of the highway, and started the sixty-mile journey through the Northern foothills of Spain. The destination was located twenty-eight miles North of La Murdedur De Surpant, the town known as the "bite of the snake".

The area had not only been infested with snakes, but it had been the hotbed for Basque terrorist activities who had struck the French and Spanish governments in raids of terror in their quest for independence. The tiny town was also the home of several loyal AIO agents who had lost their lives trying to kill Harold Gatewood.

The passenger in the right front seat was the Koldo, the National Commander of the AIO. He was on a mission to inspect the agents who were the finalists for the trip to the Dominican Republic to finally put Harold Gatewood where it belonged, in the ground. Two men, both originally from the La Merdedur De Surpant, had been tested and shown excellent skills, courage, temperament, and knowledge of terrorist activities to warrant a final look by Koldo.

They had been tested, mentally and physically, to see if they could pick up the banner of the AIO and become a quality field agent for the terrorist organization's most important mission.

The training program had lasted several months, and the four hopefuls represented the survivors of a group of sixty-three candidates who had started the elimination process. Many had been judged unqualified for this special mission due to physical limitations. Others had been deficient in their lust for killing, and were placed in more placid support positions within the organization.

Others had simply decided to quit, deciding the spy business was too rigorous, or too dangerous for their liking. They had left, to enter civilian life.

Koldo would stay at the training camp four days, assessing the final candidates and getting feedback from the trainers who had worked with them for months. He had read their progress reports, but he wanted to see the finalists in action, and look them in the eye to get a gut feeling on who would be strong enough to deal with Gatewood, as he proved to be a worthy adversary. Koldo had always thought that Harold had been lucky in his escapes from AIO agents.

The National Commander was totally frustrated with the AIO's inability to kill the ballplayer, and desperately wanted this mission to succeed. He had lost much sleep over the situation, as he knew his leadership in the organization hinged on eliminating Gatewood.

The candidates were put through tests involving hand-to-hand combat, rifle and pistol shooting, knife throwing, sword fighting, wrestling, waterboarding and pain tolerance, demolition training, and car bombing techniques. Additional assessments were made on the candidates' abilities in strangulation methods, navigation through an obstacle course while dodging live ammo fire, and tests involving how an agent would deal with potential real-life scenarios.

Koldo was especially interested in how each candidate would fare in the bloodlust killing area and wanted both of the future field agents to be retested while he was there. He knew that Gatewood was now battle-ready and would not hesitate to defend himself, as he had killed before.

At the end of the first day, Koldo had narrowed the search down to two agents, Estevo Peio, whose nickname, "El Ray Del Terror". meant "The Lightning Bolt of Terror", and "Theobaldo Gil", his cousin, whose nickname, the "Liberatdor De Mayha", meant the "The Deliverer of Mayham". Both candidates' skills were excellent, with each candidate having the advantage in several assessment areas. Ultimately, the choice boiled down to the specific plan Koldo had outlined. He had spoken to both candidates, one at a time.

"Agent Gil, you are a vastly talented agent, with skills in all areas. You will serve many missions for your fellow-Basque loyalists and prove to be a valuable asset of the AIO for many years to come. I regret to inform you that you have not chosen you for this particular mission. I am always honest with my agents, and I want to tell why you were not chosen."

Koldo had continued, "I appreciate the special skills an agent such as you brings to the table in this business. But, for this mission, for this particular target, I was looking for an agent of your skills, and who also possessed a less-revolting physical appearance. You have the skills but you are a disgusting-looking man. That is not a criticism of you."

Koldo had said, "This particular target, Harold Gatewood, is a handsome, charming, exciting man who draws the most beautiful women in the world to him like moths to a light. He also travels in circles of handsome and beautiful people. Our research has shown that agents need to be able to blend in with their surroundings. Your appearance would cause you to stand out like a sore thumb, and draw unneeded attention to your movements. "

Gil had replied, "I understand Sir. I am aware I am not a world-class, handsome man, or a male model, and I will not take the choice of my cousin as an act of rebuke for my skills. I understand what you are looking for in terms of this mission, and this target. I will stand ready to serve the AIO anytime you may need my services."

"Thank you for understanding. I will call upon you in the future. Stay ready and be patient."

"I will Sir."

Next in line was Estevo Peio. He had passed the training obstacles and was now the choice to deal with Gatewood. Koldo had called to him to enter the room. "Congratulations Estevo. You are our choice for the mission. Your mastery of the training program requirements was excellent. Your choice was based on your across the board evaluations, and on my belief that you have the killer instinct needed to eliminate a target who has brought shame on the AIO.

The National Commander had said, "One other factor in your selection was your strong genetic linkage to the Taino native people of the Dominican Republic. Your great, great, great-grandfather married his first wife, a Taino woman, when he visited the island country."

Peoi had spoken, "Yes Sir. He was a seafarer. They married and returned to Spain, settling in La Merdedur De Surpant generations ago."

Peio had continued, "I believe you mean Harold Gatewood is my target."

"Yes."

The operative had replied, "Sir, I have dreamed of killing him since I heard what he did to us in San Toro de Lidia. My distaste for him has grown over the past few years when he further disgraced the AIO by escaping our net, and helping cause the death of our agents."

"You have an excellent grasp of the past. Now, you are the instrument of revenge for the present."

"I am happy because I think you want me to kill him."

"You are correct. We want you to do that, or not come back alive."

"I will come back Sir, and he will not."

"Excellent Estevo. You will be briefed on the mission this evening, and be on a plane to Santo Domingo, Dominican Republic in the morning."

"It will be my honor Sir."

Koldo had wrapped up the details of the trips with the personnel who would help ensure that Estevo Peio had the needed items for the mission, including money, passport, and cover identity as a geneticist specializing in sugar cane development.

Knowing the mission was in good hands, Koldo had reclaimed his seat in the front, right passenger seat of the black luxury car. As the car eased out of the training facility he turned to his driver and had said, "I have said this before. I really hope that this one may finally get the job done."

On this trip Koldo took the opportunity to speak with Theobaldo Gil again. "Are you ready for the mission of your life?"

"Yes Sir."

"Do you understand what is riding on this mission?"

"Yes Sir."

"What is your understanding of the mission?"

"I am to kill Harold Gatewood."

"True, but there is more to it than that."

"What is it Sir?"

"It is the restoring of the honor of our organization.

We have allowed Harold Gatewood to make fools of us, bring ridicule upon our inability to function as terrorists, and create an opinion in the Spanish and French governments that we are not an organization that needs to be monitored. Our members are demanding that a final solution be accomplished for the Harold Gatewood situation."

"I understand. I promise I will kill him.

"I have heard that many times. Yet, he manages to survive. I want you to understand that my leadership is being questioned due to the many failures to kill Gatewood. If this mission fails I will be out as the leader of the AIO."

"Sir, I will make sure that does not happen."

"Theobaldo, I want you to understand that your failure to eliminate Gatewood will lead to your death, either by his hands, or by my order to have you killed."

"I understand. And, I will kill him. My Basque relatives and fellow patriots demand that I be successful."

"Good. I have complete confidence in you. I will place your name before the committee and recommend that you be chosen to perform "Operacion Para Romper, Operation Go For Broke."

"I will be honored Sir."

"Don't be honored. Be successful. Or, you will be killed."

"I will do it to honor our Basque people."

After mentioning that Gil would be engaging in further training to acclimate himself to the climate where Gatewood would be eliminated, Koldo entered his car, and had his driver return him to Madrid.

As he looked out the window and watched the fields and countryside pass by, Koldo wondered, "Is he the one?"

Chapter 8

A New Man

March 1

RICK OWENS WAS A NEW MAN. He had lost thirty-five pounds since he had stared jogging, and watching Aamir Jawdat for potential espionage and terrorist activities. Owens had changed his diet, concentrating on fruits, vegetables and fish, and dumping sugars, white flour, and soda pop. He had even switched from sugar-laced coffee to green tea. His concentration at work had improved, and his energy level had gone through the roof. He was in the best shape of his life.

His wife was overjoyed with the " New Owens", and constantly told him how much she was proud of him. He was now able to run a mile in a very good time, and he looked forward to his daily workout, as he had become addicted to the high he gained from the exercise regime. He relished in the idea that now he could say, "I am in really good shape. I have made some great changes in my appearance and my job performance has become much better."

He was still using the interval training approach that had allowed him to feel like an athlete again. His wife had even agreed to start working out and had enrolled in an aerobics class at their gym. The Owens family was on a health kick.

Another consistent factor in his after-work visits to the running track near their home was the ability to continue to monitor Aamir Jawdat. While many things had changed in the time since Owens had started to work out and tail Jawdat, several constants remained.

The suspected spy still sported his new, shiny, blue-and-yellow striped jogging clothes and new, matching running shoes. He still went to the tall walnut tree to the right of the banked curve of the jogging track to search for his messages from his "outside employer".

Before retrieving his messages, Aamir still looked around sheepishly to make sure no one would be watching him when he reached down to pick up a medium-sized rock from the ground. He always followed the second step of the process in a consistent manner, and had his own style of picking up a piece of paper from the ground under where the rock had been located.

Jawdat would then read the note, put the paper in his pocket, and place the rock back in its original position. He would then turn and walk back to the parking lot, in the opposite direction of Rick Olson. He would log less than one-tenth of a mile on his shiny new shoes, as he always parked close to the track.

Olson always made notes on Aamir's actions, and would always continue to walk or run around the track past the tree to the parking lot to not alert the spy that his actions were being watched. Owens was building a large file on Aamit Jawdat. Each morning following the surveillance, Owens would drive to his office with a report to discuss with his deputy director, Terry Robbins.

After reaching his destination, Owens would ride the elevator up to his office floor and settle into his corner office to ready himself for his meeting with CIO deputy director Terry Robbins.

Robbins, who had been shamed into a running program by Owens' success, had arrived early today and after some small talk they discussed the incident report.

"Terry, let's look at one of the worst spots first. The Middle East is still embroiled in the war in Syria, and the resulting migration of illegal immigrants toward Europe."

"The numbers are up because we are in the warm weather period in Europe and there is no weather danger of crossing the sea into Greece."

"Yes, that is true and there are more immigrants now than before. The political situation and war is horrible in Syria, as one can't tell who is fighting for whom. The situation still changes daily and it is hard to unravel the political relationships to determine who is actually a friend or an enemy. No one trusts anyone else. The basic mistrust in the region has been going on for centuries."

"It is still hard to determine which terrorist group is gaining or losing strength Sir."

"True. All of the countries are also dealing with related terrorist threats. Lebanon, Qatar, Egypt, Iran, Iraq, and all of the rest are in, facing, or causing potential turmoil."

"What about the other players Sir?"

"Egypt can be added to that list. There are terrorism problems and immigrants are coming from there now also."

"Who else in active in the region?"

"Rick, the problem in the Middle East has caused a worldwide crisis, as immigrants are fleeing many countries."

"What about Russia's actions?"

"Russia is still wielding influence. We in America suffered from weak leadership in the presidency over the last eight years. The policy in Libya caused this situation. We still find ourselves suffering from those factors."

"Is there any good news for this situation?"

"Yes. Now Turkey has changed and is more supportive of our efforts. They have even jailed journalists who have falsely reported on the country's situation, and are now controlling the news outlets. They are now passing laws that help fight immigration into their country. Turkey itself has been the victim of several terrorist attacks. They have seen the light."

"When it hits their country many have a change in their attitude toward illegal immigration. It would be nice if the whole situation would go away but it will not. The resulting problems have changed the world."

"It is a challenge Sir."

"Let's move on to Europe. As we discussed, the illegal immigrant invasion from the Middle East has altered Europe forever. Germany is now suffering from their ill-fated decision to welcome all immigrants at the expense of their national interests."

"Yes, they were the first to do so."

Owens continued, "Yes. They needed to reboot their population as their birth rate was falling, and in a few years they would need more people to man their economy. But, the decision has been taken at the expense of their culture. Now the German people are upset, angry, and want to reverse the decisions of their leader."

"Yes. She lost the election and is out. The new man in charge will have to clean up her mess."

"True, but it will be difficult, and take time. They now face the influx of immigrants who do not want to assimilate into the German culture, and want to impose their own beliefs on the country. And, there have been incidents of lawlessness, and attacks and serial rapes by groups of migrants on German women."

"It is no wonder that the German citizens are upset."

"Yes. The country now has to deal with terrorists who want to create havoc."

"What have they done to shore up their border security and protective abilities?"

Owens answered, "They are now using good tactics, and the German people seem to have the resolve to help address the problems. They have started to send immigrants back to Africa when they arrive by boat. They are putting a limit on the number of illegals they will now take. If the politicians will keep a stiff backbone then there will be progress. If not, then kiss Germany goodbye."

"I agree Sir"

"Germany's neighbor, Austria, is now facing problems."

"Yes, immigrants are being smuggled into the country in railroad cars. They need to get with the program or they will be overrun."

"Spain continues to face their economic and internal terrorist problems. The AIO is still operating. We know they have sent operatives to train with the TCPLM in Columbia. We also know that they are beefing up the number of their agents in order to forcibly attempt to gain independence for their members."

"What is being done in opposition to the AIO?"

"King Alfonso IV has given his full support to fight the resistance forces. Also, the stoppage of the drug shipments from the Dominican Republic into Europe has really hurt the AIO's cash flow. They will be concentrating on that rather than stemming the immigration flow."

"King Alfonso is a good ally for America."

"Yes he is. In England, the people voted to leave the European Confederation and stand for their national unity. They have faced terrorist problems due to the changing complexion of their population. London especially has been impacted by the illegal immigration from the Middle East. They continue to be our strongest partner in Europe but they have severe problems."

"I agree Rick. England has suffered from mass immigration of people who do not consider themselves as British. They do not relate to the country's history, or desire to acclimate into English society. They want to remake the country."

"Sir, France has been rocked with terrorist attacks. They have a severe problem on their hands. Terrorist groups have them in their sights and have threatened many more attacks. They now plan on building a safety wall around the Eiffel Tower to protect it from a terrorist attacks. Sir, they have recognized that they are a target and have been forced to deal with the problem."

"Yes, with help from the world community they may be able to keep that situation under control. I hate to say this but Germany, France, England, and the rest of Europe has brought this illegal immigrant invasion upon their own countries by not opposing it from the start."

"The same situation exists in Belgium. They have been hit hard in Brussels on multiple occasions. They are now taking the problem very seriously."

"Yes, they were unprepared before they were hit."

"Switzerland has yet to be affected by terrorism, but they are on the radar screen as a warning was just issued by several terrorist groups."

"They are pretty isolated."

"True, but they only have a volunteer civil defense plan, and have no military."

"They would be prime target if the country were infiltrated."

Owens continued on the European rundown. The Eastern European countries have closed down their borders, and are not allowing immigrants to enter. If they can keep out the illegals they will be okay."

"They will be one of the few countries who will be. Even Greece now wants to stop the illegal flow of bodies. If it can't be done they want to leave the federation."

"Italy is now being impacted. Even Lake Como has illegals housed near the town."

"I am sure that is causing fear for the rich and famous people who live there. I believe that Italy will start refusing to accept illegal immigrants."

"Yes the rich are facing what we middle-class people face. Europe has lost it culture, and traditions."

"What about Sweden?"

Owens answered, "They are now experiencing problems from illegals they allowed in their country. There have been many attacks o Swedish women who have been going about their everyday life."

"What about Finland and the rest of that area?"

"It will have problems if they admit illegals. Finland has not been hurt yet."

"That area is a cold, out-of-the-way part of the world, yet they are vulnerable."

"True. Even Asia has its own problems. China is addressing an economic downturn, and is flexing its muscles in the South China Sea by building islands on top of coral reefs and claiming the area as their own, thus violating prior agreements. Japan, which is also in a bad way economically, South Korea, Viet Nam, and the Philippines are being impacted by China's actions. North Korea has now threatened use first strikes with their nukes. China has refused to allow any illegal immigrants into their country. "

"I know that China has shown a strong military presence in the area. They just sent a naval ship through Japanese waters near Okinawa, and sent fighter jets through other countries air space. They now control the South China Sea and have pushed our influence all the way back to Guam."

"Yes, we have watched them develop into a world military power. Now, they send flights of planes over Japan that have nuclear delivery abilities."

"China is not very appreciative for our efforts in helping them become accepted into the world community, the World Trade Association, and to become a trading partner with us."

"Yes, a partner who enjoys a massive trade advantage over us, as we buy all of their cheap-labor manufactured goods. We can't compete trade-wise because of their currency manipulation."

"True. Is Russia continuing to be a problem?"

"Yes. Russia is being hurt by the crash in oil prices. They have become a stronger player in the Middle East as a result of that problem. The recent decision by the oil producing countries in the Middle East to cut production is a result of Russia's influence."

"What about Central America Rick?"

"They are sending immigrants through Mexico to America. That could get worse."

"What is happening in the Caribbean?"

"After stopping the drug flow from Venezuela for a short period, the Columbian drugs are once again being shipped through the Dominican Republic from Venezuela. We will talk about that in a minute."

"What about Cuba?"

"The administration opened up relations with them, and it has been a mixed bag of results. It looks like the Bertalina government will be friendlier than his predecessors, but there is still an anti-American sentiment that has been hard to overcome."

"What about South America?"

Owens added, "Our reports show that economic problems still exist in Argentina. They are suffering from inflation. The other countries like Chile, Bolivia, Uruguay, Paraguay, and Peru have shown very little progress in climbing out of poverty. Brazil is somewhat impacted by Columbia's drug situation. Many countries are close to collapse and martial law, which would be terrible for us as their people would migrate North towards America, and cross our borders."

"What about Columbia?"

"They have been working with us on the drug situation. We have been assisting them in their program of eradicating cocaine crops and paying the locals to grow substitute crops like bananas."

"What about the drug cartels?"

"The Carmelo Cartel, headed by the Candy Man, Rafael Carmelo, has not been cooperating and has still increased production to flood the market with cocaine, gain market share, and permanently drive their competitors out of business. The Mountain Producers Cartel, supposedly headed by Lino Pascual, has been doing the same."

"Sir, have we uncovered any new clues about who may actually head up the Mountain Producers?"

"No. We think it is a powerful man, named Mateo Amon, the father of Harold Gatewood's love interest Sofia Amon, who died when they visited Ella Se Cayo, is still running the operation behind the scenes. We had Jack Taylor and Harold Gatewood in Venezuela trying to find out his identity. Word has it that Mateo Amon would like to kill Gatewood. "

"Has the Colombian government made any progress?"

"Yes, they were successful. Columbia is still continuing to fight the TCPLM. They have an agreement with Venezuela to ship the cocaine from there to the Dominican Republic. The drugs are then shipped to America and Canada."

"How does that work?"

"Venezuela is given a cut of the profits to look the other way and let the shipments go through the country."

"It is a real criminal enterprise."

"Yes. Everyone takes a cut, including the Nazoa government, the military, and the TCPLM, who even have an office in Caracas."

"Is there any way to stop or lessen the influx of drugs into America?"

Owens replied, "We are balancing our actions in Venezuela, as we have spoken on this topic before. When Gatewood's Venezuelan lover, Luisa Gaicia worked for the TCPLM she was able to feed Gatewood information on the schedules, distribution routes, and receiving areas for the drugs. We did very well in terms of stopping the flow of drugs until she went to America with Gatewood. She has been killed by one of Gatewood's groupies so the drug pipeline to the Dominican Republic is again open."

Owens continued, "We are still trying to control the supply of cocaine coming into America, lessen Venezuela's assistance to terrorist groups that threaten our borders, and keep the Nazoa government in check as best as we can."

"What are the most recent reports?"

"Sabotage in some of the cocaine fields in Columbia may keep supply down. Inflation is still at eleven hundred percent or higher in Venezuela. The country has almost tripled the money supply. The currency had to be changed by adding a zero on the bills because of the devaluation, and money needed to buy goods will not even fit into a wallet now because too many bills of worthless denominations. The situation is the same as in German Weimer government in the 1920's. Venezuelan women travel to Columbia to sell their hair for money."

"It is a terrible situation."

"It is. The people are experiencing food shortages. They have attacked supermarkets and ambushed food deliver trucks, butchered dogs, cats, and horses for food, and now are forced by the government to work in the fields a day or two a week to help fight the shortages. They now grow food in every spare patch of dirt in the cities. Many travel to Columbia to buy food. Medical supplies are almost non-existent. Sanitary conditions in the hospital are disgusting. The situation is worsening just as we feared."

"Yes Terry. We still have measures we can do, and our backup plan is in place. We have already ordered the families of our consulate employees to return to America."

"What can we try next?"

"We plan on buying more oil from Venezuela. We will also try to hold down production here in the United States. We will work with their lenders like China to soften their credit terms or rewrite their loans. Perhaps Harold Gatewood could help, as his ex-father-in-law is Guo Gang, the leader of China."

"He married into a highly-respected family."

"Yes, he was close to the family until his wife Akemi was killed by the Yakuza crime family."

"Gatewood has gone through misery the last four years. Now his love Luisa is dead, and he is being stalker by her killer, Susana Richards."

"Yes, Ms. Richards was just placed on our most wanted list. Hopefully, Venezuela's trade partners can urge them to get the country under control."

"Sir, that goal will be hard to accomplish due to the corruption at all levels of government in their country."

"True. We will try to work with Venezuela, despite their actions and attitudes. But, we may have to support a candidate to gain office and oust Nazoa from power. We can't take military means to remove him but we can try more subtle means to achieve our mission.

The Venezuelan government is already considering on trial for crimes against the country. We believe he would flee the country, like the Nazis Adolf Eichmann and Joseph Mengele did when they went to South America. Nazoa has already thrown some of his critics in jail, the same as Abraham Lincoln did in the Civil War. It looks like revolt and bloodshed may be in store for Venezuela."

"We can use humanitarian aid in the meantime."

"That is true Terry. But that action is a temporary fix to a permanent problem. We need to keep the cocaine supply entering America at its current level and not let the cartels and Venezuela flood the market. Once they drive out their competitors through cheapening the product, they would control price and supply. But, we have to be mindful not to destroy too much supply or Venezuela would lose some of the income stream, and force them into a worse financial position."

"How will we address the problem if we can't destroy some of the product?"

"In the past America has bought drugs to learn the identity of the cartels, producers, and their shipment dates. We might have to do that again."

"That is politically risky for any administration."

"True. We have several issues to juggle."

"What else are we planning to implement Sir?"

"We are hopeful that we can find out the information about the TCPLM's drug shipments out of Venezuela. That would be a big boost for our monitoring the cocaine supply. If we can't uncover those shipment dates and times then we will have to divert more American dollars and send more covert agents to the help out the effort."

"Is Venezuela doomed Rick?"

"Yes, unless something unseen happens to turn the situation around. Socialism has failed once again."

"They are idiots. Socialism has never worked."

"Yes, they are Terry. We need to take precautions on how to stop the cancer from spreading from Venezuela into Central America, and then into Mexico. Mexico is the last stop before our last line of defense, our borders, are compromised. The illegals would stream in even faster than they are now, and totally ruin our country."

"We have the report for Mexico here Sir. It says that the drug cartels are still out of control, and killing each other. Violence in Mexico is rampant. Murders and kidnapping are at an all-time high. The decline in oil production has caused financial problems in the country and taken the value of the peso to a dangerously low level. Illegal immigration into America has exploded to new highs, and nothing is being done to stem the tide."

"Yes. Place that at the feet of the man currently in the White House. Luckily he will be gone in a few months. He has put the country in peril to gain enough illegal alien votes to sway the next election and keep his liberal party in control. The country is in decline. They are afraid of one of our candidates for the presidency as he wants to build a wall to keep out the illegals, and tax Mexico with a tariff on cars manufactured there and sold in America."

"Yes, there will be an attempt to have every illegal alien vote. And, I am sure that there will be election fraud. We need a nationalist for president, a person, man or woman, who will stop this insanity from continuing."

"Terry, we have dead people voting multiple times, sanctuary cities that do not stop vote fraud because it costs only a few dollars for an illegal to buy fake identification cards. Sanctuary cities do not deport illegal aliens or enforce the law against them. Fake or missing registration applications that are needed for the right to vote are rampant."

"Is there a way to stop the sanctuary cities?"

"Yes, that is easy. The law already exists that federal money can be cut off to the cities if the cities do not follow federal law. No political party can stop the law from being enforced."

"Is there enough political resolve and money to build a wall on the border of Mexico?"

"Yes there is enough money. A tax can be placed on the money sent by workers in the United States that is sent back to Mexico to easily do that. As far as having enough political resolve to do, that depends on which political party and candidate gets elected."

"We have other issues to address the many failures of the last eight years, including national health insurance failures, the climate change hoax, and the economy."

"And, the most important problem of all Terry, is illegal immigration."

"Yes Sir, it will be an important election."

"By the way Terry, do you know if Aamir Jawdat has continued his routine in passing information to the waitress at the restaurant?"

"Yes he is. We have agents monitoring his actions, both there and at the training camp outside Washington. D.C., in Virginia. We are completing a file on him, and the entire cell. We are identifying them one by one and monitoring what they are up to. We are using HUMIT tactics. We also have secured search warrants and are ready to move when the time is right. Sir, we could hit a homerun on this investigation, if we don't wait too long to act."

"Keep me posted. We will spring the trap when the timing is right."

"I will Sir."

"Rick, we spoke about Luisa Gaicia's murder in Mexico. He went through another similar event in the Dominican Republic on is last mission for us. Poor Gatewood. Trouble is his constant companion."

"It certainly is Rick. He is a survivor though."

"Rick, what is he doing now that he is officially out of baseball?"

"He is managing his business interests. He still lives in Gibson City, Illinois. He is living a quiet lifestyle."

"That is what he needs. He has been through the wringer the last few years."

"Yes. He has done some very nice work for us. I do hope that he does not become involved in any more dangerous events. It has been a miracle he has not been eliminated. He is a marked man, one who should retire from his service for us."

"Do you think he will ever work for us again?"

"Despite him being a good operative, I hope he retires. The odds are stacking up against him. I do not want to attend his funeral."

Chapter 9

"I love my new profession"

March 4

THE BEAUTIFUL YOUNG WOMAN TURNED OVER IN HER LOUNGE CHAIR in order to let the hot sun hit her back, as she wanted to make sure her tan would be the same on both sides of her body. She then reached down and picked up her hollow-stemmed glass of red merlot wine and sipped a mouthful of the delicious liquid.

After putting her glass down on the cement that surrounded her swimming pool she readjusted her sunglasses and thought, "I never that I would be doing this type of work. But, the transition into it seemed so easy. I love my new profession. The money is fabulous and I do not mind doing what I do as it gives me pleasure. I can pretend to be anyone, or anything, I want. "

She then closed her eyes, felt the sun's heat penetrating into back and thought about how she had reached this point. It had developed by accident but the feeling of satisfaction had been immediate. She thought about her unusual path into the trash removal business.

It had started by accident in her home town. Billly Watson, the local mailman, dressed in all his blue and gray, postal-uniform splendor, had walked into the local convenience store and handed a packet of mail to the attractive brunette behind the front counter. "Good morning Susana."

"Good morning Billy. What do you have for me today?"

"There are several letters and a package for you. The note on the cover says "media mail rates", so it must be a book."

"Great, I have been waiting for this package."

"What is the book about Susana?"

"It is about Harold Gatewood, the handsome and famous baseball player."

"You told me he was your favorite player."

"Yes, and I am president of his fan club."

"How many members are in the club?"

"Just one so far, myself. Would you like to join?"

"Maybe later. You have a good day."

"Thanks. You too Billy."

Susana had torn open the package and taken out the book she had waited so patiently to receive. Now, the moment of excitement had arrived. She was delighted that the book had been delivered so quickly. She had paid extra postage to make sure it arrived as soon as possible. She read each page, absorbing the details about Harold Gatewood in her mind.

She had read quietly in between waiting on customers who came into the store. She had hoped that no more customers would buy anything today, as she wanted to be alone with her book, and its details about her desired lover, Harold Gatewood. She was perplexed with the book's details about Gatewood, as it painted a much different picture than what she had always heard and read about him in past.

She did not understand how the publisher could write such lies about the man she planned on catching, enticing into bed, and then showering with love and affection.

When she had read what was written on page thirty-eight she threw the book on the front store counter and said, "That's it. I will not let them get away with this nonsense." She then turned on her computer and did an online search for the Placer de los Lectores book publishing company in New York City, New York. She entered the company website and read the review about the book on Gatewood. She became more incensed with each word.

She had then clicked on the employment page to check the opportunities with the company. The openings listed were for a copy editor, a graphic artist, a proofreader, a ghost writer, a security guard, a janitor, a legal secretary, and an accountant. She thought for a moment and then said, "Yes, that will work."

She had then filled out the online employment application for janitorial opportunity, hit the send button, and smiled.

She had been positive she would be hired, and made calls to a friend of hers who specialized in selling fake identification cards. She would pay four hundred dollars for a set of id's that included a fake copies of a birth certificate, driver's license, social security number, copies of utility bills, and a health club membership card. These tools would help her become a proud employee of the Placer de los Lectores book publishing company.

She then planned to use her accumulated vacation and sick leave and take a month off. That timeframe would allow her ample time to drive to New York, rent a cheap furnished apartment, brush up on information related to the best commercial janitorial supplies in the industry, and learn about the company and its employees. The company website mentioned the three most important employees in the company, CEO Gerald Anderson, Vice-President of Operations Grady Elliott, and Senior Marketing Representative Loren Melnor.

She would learn all about the three key men in the company, including personal information, their interests, their families, their employment history, their background, and their future goals. She would master the details and use them in her interview, an action which would ensure her being hired as the janitor of the company's dreams.

Then she would make the company, and the three employees, pay the price for ripping off Gatewood and his reputation. She would do it with pleasure, as she would allow anyone to soil the reputation of the man she loved, and planned to marry. Soon, she would be Mrs. Harold Gatewood.

She smiled, and took another sip of merlot, and thought about how her plan had unfolded once she had arrived in New York City. She remembered how they were always smiling when she would see them at the New York City headquarters of the of the Placer de los Lectores book publishing company. The book on Harold Gatewood's life story had been published and had shot to the top of the best seller's list. The company was raking in profits hand over fist, and the three key men in the organization, President Gerald Atkinson, Vice-President of Operations Grady Elliott, and marketing whiz Loren Melnor were gloating over the bonanza they were raking into their own coffers.

Susana Richards' original plan was to take her thirty-day accumulated vacation, go to New York City, work for the publishing company, and administer the old-fashioned, brutal methods of score-settling and revenge that her ancestors on her mother's side of the family had practiced for many years. She would right the wrongs that the publishing company, and in particular the three men she held accountable for the fraud and damages heaped upon Harold Gatewood, the man she loved and would spend the rest of her life with in matrimonial bliss.

Her plans had been delayed by a longer-than-anticipated hiring process. But, she had quickly molded into her employment position and was enjoying free reign of the office building. She worked the five to one a.m. shift, and had used her access to the offices of upper management team to discover the true extent of the fraud committed against Harold Gatewood. The company, and its three "superstars" who had master minded the disgraceful actions, were now flying high. Susana was determined to take actions to set the record straight.

President Gerald Atkinson, abuser-in-chief, called his two fellow-partners-in-crime, and had said, "Grady and Loren, please come to my office. I have the latest sales figures on the Gatewood best seller. Bring your calculators, as our regular profits, and our slush-fund bonanza figures are sky high."

Grady Elliott and Loren Melnor had then entered the office with smiles on their faces that stretched from ear-to-ear.

"Welcome book-publishing Comrades. We pulled a fast one on Gatewood and the profits are piling up. I want to show you our latest haul."

"Yes, we pulled the best fraudulent scam yet. What are the figures?" Elliott and Melnor's eyes bugged out with the totals.

Atkinson had then spoken, "Yes, we have trained our marketing reps to operate with reckless abandon, and use high-pressure, unscrupulous, deceptive marketing tactics."

Elliott then chimed in, "Yes, and we have trained our billing and finance department to ignore all requests for information about the fraud, over-billing on the clients' accounts, and to not honor any discounts or credits our marketing people have fraudulently promised."

Atkinson said, "I want to thank both of you for helping me mold a corrupt, fraudulent, and self-serving company."

Elliott and Melnor had agreed, "Here, here. It shows what teamwork, and fraudulent collusion, can accomplish."

"Yes, my friends, let's drink to that."

The three co-harts in crime then hoisted their glasses in celebration for the fraud they had committed.

After chugging down their bubbly glasses of liquid, Melnor had looked at the label on the bottle and said, "Gerald, this champagne costs seven thousand dollars a bottle."

"Yes, and after we commit more fraud on Gatewood we can afford the really expensive stuff."

The comments had caused the three men to laugh hysterically, and walk to the office windows to look out upon the lights of New York City and pledge that they would continue their fraudulent actions in the future, and shear other sheep who signed up for their services in the book publishing business.

She remembered how she had entered the room, unnoticed by the gloating threesome. She had dressed in traditional Native American clothes of the nineteenth century. She had applied turquoise and white-colored war paint on her cheeks, and forehead. She had inched toward the three men as they continued to pat themselves on the back for the crimes they had accomplished.

She had then lassoed Atkinson from behind, jerked the rope, and pulled him toward the floor. On the way down he hit his head on the corner of his dark, mahogany-colored desk, which caused blood to flow form the now-present gash at the back of his head. Elliott and Melnor had stood in stunned silence as Atkinson, encased in the rope, lay bleeding on the floor.

Susana had then pointed the pistol she now held in her hand at the two men, told Melnor to close the office drapes, and motioned for both of them to sit down in the chairs next to the desk. When they failed to do so, she had said, "Sit down now, or I will use this pistol to end your miserable, fraud-filled lives."

After obediently sitting down the men had remained silent, too taken aback to say or do anything. Susana then had thrown another rope to Melnor and told him to get up, and to tie up and gag Elliott. She then had walked to Atkinson, stopped, and kicked him the ribs. He groaned in pain. She then walked to Melnor, hit him in the back of the head with her pistol, then tied and gaged him in similar fashion as Elliott.

She had then walked to the windows behind the desk, kicked Atkinson in the ribs once again, and lifted him to his feet. She had helped him shuffle to the wall on the left of the desk. She had tied his arms to the tall, heavy bookcase on the wall and walked back to the blue gym bag she had carried when she had entered the room. She had then taken out a large, long, sharp knife and walked to Atkinson. She had then stuffed a handkerchief in his mouth and ripped the front of his shirt, causing its buttons to fly in several directions.

She then stepped forward and brandished the knife. She then turned to the two men bound and gagged in the chairs and said, "Watch this." She then cut into Atkinson's chest, peeling off thin layers of skin in surgeon-like precision, as he struggled to scream in pain.

She had smiled and looked at Elliott and Melnor. She then turned and slid her knife blade under the front hairline on Atkinson's head. She then peeled her knife towards the back of his head. She then held her prize, Atkinson's scalp, in her hand high above her head.

She had then moved toward the two men and suddenly turned and threw her knife. After sailing through the air, the knife found home in Atkinson's heart, causing instant death. She danced in circles, chanting verses she had learned from her mother as a little girl, until she reached the hanging corpse. She turned and spoke to Elliott and Melnor. "That is what we do to people who cheat other people in my home town of Scalp, Minnesota."

She had then placed Atkin's scalp on the right corner of his desk, facing the entry door. She had then looked again at Elliott and Melnor, who both had terror in their eyes. She said, "My ancestors did that to Custer at Little Bighorn on June 25, 1876. Which one of you want to be next?"

Both men had sat motionless, frozen in panic.

She had then performed an elimination process named eeny-meeny-miny-moe, and had then had settled on Elliott. She had walked him to the wall of on the left side of the office and tied him to the tall, large bookcase that was a twin of the one on the other side of the room where Atkinson's corpse now hung. She had then tied him up in the same fashion as she had done with her first victim, and proceeded to perform her patented same skin-removal process.

When done, she had placed Elliott's scalp on the desk next to Atkinson's and did her circular, celebratory dance over to Melnor. She had then said, "I have been saving a special surprise for you because you insulted my love, my future husband, Harold Gatewood, when you talked to him and then suggested what was written in that pathetic book of lies."

She then ushered him to the large, rectangular desk in the corner of the room. She had him lie down, and she proceeded to tie his arms and legs to the support braces on the underside of the table. She then repeatedly struck him in the groin area with the handle of her long-bladed knife. She then performed her classic skin slicing ritual. Next on the menu of terror was the traditional scalping and removal of the victim's sparse quantity of hair.

She had then danced in circles to the desk, and placed Melnor's scalp next to the others. She then danced her way back to Melnor, chanting her ritual words. She pulled his now-hair-barren head up from where it hung chin down against his chest, and said, "Look at what I have for you."

His eyes had then focused on a large tomahawk that rested in Susana's hand. She had said, "You will have the pleasure of seeing this fly toward your head, hit you between the eyes, and end your life immediately. As you see it coming toward you I want you to remember what you have done to my future husband, Harold Gatewood. I also want you to know that your corpse will rot for two more days, as tomorrow starts the weekend and no janitorial service will be done until the start of the week."

Melnor's eyes were then wide-open and frozen with fear.

Susana had then backed up and stopped fifteen feet from the victim. She had performed two mock throws, each of which caused Melnor's heart to race. Finally, she had said, "Get ready Melnor, here it comes. Be sure to watch it as it makes its way to your face and hits you in a painful manner." Her throwing arm thrust forward and the tomahawk flew through the air, turning end-over-end until it found home between the victim's eyes, and split Melnor's head in a shattering blow.

Susana had then danced in circles around the office for four laps, chanting her victory as she went. She then walked to the bathroom of the luxurious office, washed the blood from her face that had splattered upon her when she had done the killings, and picked up her small bag. She then took a final look at her work, smiled, and in a parting act of her disdain for the victims, spit at the three men. She then said, "I have righted the wrongs of these three men in the same way as my ancestors did at Little Bighorn. I love you Harold Gatewood."

She had then followed Harold and his lover Luisa Gaicia to Gibson City. After spying on the lovebirds she had kidnapped Luisa and ordered Harold to go to the baseball diamond by the high school as she "had something to show him."

When he arrived they started to talk.

"Susana, did you kill those men in New York City?"

"Oh, New York City. Yes, I was there for a while."

"What happened?"

"I had to correct a situation at the Placer de los Lectores book publishing company for you."

"What did you do?"

"I took tribal vengeance on the three men who insulted your honor in print, and made them regret their cruel and disdainful misdeeds."

"Susana, why did you kill those three men?"

"I killed Atkinson first. Then I killed Elliott in a similar manner. And, I saved the best until last. I killed Melnor as the grand finale because he mistreated you in person."

"How could you torture, scalp, and mutilate them?"

"The acts of revenge were needed to wash away the lies they printed about you."

"That was cruel."

"No, it was revenge, and justice."

"How long have you been here?"

"I have been scouting the area for three days."

"Scouting for what?"

"For the perfect place of course."

"Perfect place for what?"

"The perfect place to separate Luisa from your life."

"What?"

"The perfect place to make sure Luisa exits your life."

"You can't do that."

"Of course I can. It is our destiny."

"There is no destiny for you and I."

"Oh yes Harold. We will be together forever."

"No we won't."

"Harold, you need to let me take care of things and then we can be together."

"Why am I here Susana?"

"I am at the scene where many of your talents got a start, and where you had many nice moments."

Harold continued to do as he was instructed. He stood at home plate and looked in horror at the backstop. Luisa was tied to the wire screen. Her arms were outstretched and her legs were bound together. She was tied in a manner of a person being crucified on a cross. Her head was hanging down, her chin on her chest. He called her name and she raised her head, and looked at him, her eyes begging for help. She had been beaten. Blood had dried on her face, near her nostrils.

Harold's phone rang, and a voice said, "There she is, in all of her glory. Luisa and I had a nice conversation. Eventually, she saw things my way and agreed to be here like this, waiting for you."

Harold looked around. He scanned the bleachers and area behind the backstop. He then looked at track area behind the dugouts. No one was in the area. He wanted to go to Luisa but dared not do so as he had been warned to stay put.

"Harold, how do you like how Luisa looks now?"

"You are very cruel Susana."

"Perhaps Harold. But, I wanted to get your attention."

"You have. Let her go."

"No, she must pay for making you chase all over Mexico to find her."

"Please, let her go."

"I think not my love."

"Can I go to the fence to talk to her?"

"Yes, I want you to do that."

Harold walked to the fence, hugged Luisa as best as he cold, and spoke softly to her. "It will be fine honey. I am here."

Susana's voice came over a speaker that was located nearby. "That was very touching Harold. But, that is not going to happen. Kiss her."

Harold did as ordered. He kissed her, wiped the dried blood from her nose, and told her that he was going to free her. A voice was heard again, "Yes Harold, I want you to hold her."

Harold quickly untied the ropes that bound Luisa to the wire of the backstop and held her in his arms. She meekly kissed him, as she was exhausted physically. He returned the kiss and told her things were going to be alright.

Susana's voice was then heard. "Kiss her one more time Harold."

He kissed Luisa and told her he loved her. Susana's voice was again heard. "That was your goodbye kiss." A rifle shot raced through the air, and entered Luisa's head, splattering blood, bone, and brain tissue on Harold's face, arms, and hands.

Luisa's body went limp, and Harold, holding her in his arms, slumped to the ground. He held her lifeless body to his chest and started to sob. They both had made long journeys to be together again. It was not right their future together would end like this, her dead in his arms, both sitting on the ground by the backstop.

Harold heard a car engine start, looked at the far end of the football field, and saw a car speed away in a Northerly direction from Gibson City. Susana's voice was again heard on the phone, "I will see you soon Harold."

Susana leaned down and grabbed her glass of merlot. She then laughed about the incident at the ball diamond and continued to think about Harold Gatewood.

When she had found out the Harold was headed to the Dominican Republic she had sent him a note, and then had boarded the same flight as he had scheduled. She remembered how he had not recognized her as she sat next to him on the plane, pretending to be an international lawyer named Linda Westmorland.

She had then arranged for them to meet. She smiled when she thought about how wonderfully Harold had treated her when he was courting her. She remembered his words and actions like it was yesterday.

When they had landed, they made arrangements to meet. When she left the terminal she had grabbed Harold's hand, squeezed it tightly, and said, "It was nice to meet Harold. Please call me."

She had then leaned in and kissed him gently on the lips, and then walked out into the sunshine.

Susana took a deep breath and remembered how romantic and charming he was in person. He was even better than she had hoped.

She had booked a room in the same hotel where he was staying so that they could be close. When he picked her up for their first date he had been so cute. She remembered his words, and how quickly they had become lovers.

She had opened her hotel room door and smiled. She was dressed in a pale blue dress that stopped at her shoulders, had long earrings that drooped two inches below her ear lobes, and wore a matching light-pale-blue ribbon in her hair. She wore light-blue shoes with one-inch heels. Harold's eyes followed her legs up from her shoes and to the bottom of her dress, which stopped two inches above her knees.

He then looked at Linda and said, "Wow ! You look great."

Harold's unexpected shout of approval startled Linda but she soon broke out into laughter as she realized, one, that he did it to make her relax and laugh, and two, he meant it, as she could tell from his smile and his eyes. She threw her arms around Gatewood's neck, hugged him tightly, and whispered in his ear, "That was the nicest, most surprising hello I have ever received. I loved it."

Harold laughed and said, "I meant it. You look spectacular."

She hugged him again. Little did he know that she had dreamed of this moment for a very long time.

Harold said, "Where are you taking me tonight Linda?"

"I know that you eat light, like salads, don't eat too much meat other than chicken or turkey, and drink lots of water. I know you like to work out, and the results are obvious. So, I thought we would go to a traditional Dominican Republic restaurant and you can order what you like."

"How do you know that about me Linda?"

"You are a very famous man. You are a baseball player, a business and farm owner, are intelligent, have a doctoral degree, love the outdoors, and like to travel on hunting and fishing trips to beautiful places in the world. I know that you are a Renaissance man Harold Gatewood."

"Thanks for the compliments."

"I am the president of your fan club and I have been doing research on you."

"You flatter me too much."

"I mean it Harold. I liked you from the first minute we met on the plane."

"I liked you also. I was hoping you would be sitting in the empty seat next to me when you were walking down the aisle."

"So was I."

"Well Linda, look how nice it has worked out."

She giggled and said that she agreed. She then suggested they head to the restaurant.

"Should I drive tonight Linda?"

"No. It is only a short distance. It will be nice to walk, plus we can talk on the way."

They held hands, talked, and laughed on the way to the Club de Cena Dominicana, the Dominicana Supper Club.

Harold asked, "What kind of food is on the menu?"

"Excepcionial y tradicional cocina Dominicana"

"Exceptional and traditional Dominican cuisine, correct?"

"Excellent Harold. You speak Spanish very well."

Gatewood laughed and said, "Linda, my high school Spanish teacher would disagree with you."

"Why?"

"Because after two years of it in high school she told me that she could write all the Spanish I knew on a postage stamp an she would have room left over."

"Oh stop it Harold. No one is that grammatically challenged after two years of classes. What did you tell her after she said that ridiculous comment?"

He laughed and said, "What could I say? It was true."

They entered and were ushered to their table. They talked for several minutes and were finally ready to order. Linda ordered guisados, which consisted of meat, fish, bell peppers, onion, garlic, celery, and olives, a house salad, and coffee with cream and sugar. Harold followed with moro de guandules, yellow rice with peas, olives and onions. He asked the waitress to substitute chicken for the traditional pork. He also had a house salad, and ice water to drink.

They talked and ate, being careful not to make a mistake of spilling their food or drinks. Linda recounted how one of her girlfriends would always try to make her laugh when they were eating. Harold told the story of one of his friends who had done the same thing. They both agreed that that was what friends were for. Harold asked about her childhood.

Linda said her parents had spilt up when she was young. The family was living in Nebraska at the time. After the divorce Linda moved to Brunswick, Maine where she stayed from age eleven through high school. She then went to college in California, and law school in Arizona, as she had mentioned on the plane.

Harold told her that he had spent all of his school years, kindergarten through high school, in Gibson City. He then went to his undergraduate and master's college years close to his home, and then started playing baseball. He earned a doctorate while he was still playing in the big leagues.

After dinner they danced to slow music at the restaurant, but avoided the fast ones, as Linda was wearing short heels and did not want to sprain her ankle. During the last slow dance Linda whispered in Harold's ear, "I have had fun tonight Harold."

"So have I Linda."

"Harold, I want you to take me back to the hotel now. I want to make love with you all night long."

Harold was surprised by her comment and looked into her eyes. She kissed him passionately, after which Linda honored her promise to take Harold to supper and paid the bill. Harold left the tip and they walked back to the hotel, talking and holding hands.

They rode the elevator up to the sixth floor, turned the key in the lock, shut the door, and kissed their way to the bed. Harold unzipped her dress in the back, and they both laughed as it made a "swoosh" sound as it slid down her body to the floor. They took turns helping each other out of their clothes, and were soon in bed.

They talked for a short time and then made love several times during the night, being interrupted by short naps in between the glorious events.

The next morning Linda was up early, getting ready for work. When it was time to leave she walked to the bed, sat down, and stroked Harold's hair. He responded and said, "Good morning."

She returned the comment, and then said that last night had been the nicest night of her life. Harold said that he had loved being with her and that she was even more wonderful that he had hoped. She said that she needed to go to work and that she would like to see him after supper tonight if he did not have other plans. He said that he did not have any plans and asked her what time was good for her.

"Nine tonight, after I finish work and clean up."

"Do you want to go out?"

"No, I want to stay in with you. Please come to my room."

"Okay. Do you need a ride to work?"

"No. My law firm is just down the street, at the intersection of Guillermo and Campos streets, Suite C."

"Okay. I will see you tonight."

Linda turned and started for the door. Harold sat up in bed and lovingly threw his pillow at Linda, softly hitting her in the back. Started, she turned around, saw the pillow on the floor, started to laugh, and ran to the bed, jumped on Harold with the pillow in her hands and started to gently smack him with it. Soon both of them were laughing like school children.

She stopped and kissed him passionately, then said, "I love being with you Harold."

He returned the compliment, and then the kiss, and soon they were embraced in a passionate love-making session once again. After twenty minutes, she said that she had to go to work as she was late. She kissed him gently and said, "We can pick this up again when I see you tonight." She then walked to the door. She stopped, turned around, smiled, and said, "I will see you at nine tonight Harold. Have a fun day." She then blew him a kiss and headed off to work.

He could not wait for her to return from work and be with him in the evening.

Susana smiled, took another sip of merlot and remembered how much she had enjoying making love with Harold. They became constant companions until Harold became suspicious of her faux employment and movements during the day. She knew he had found her safe house and the items she needed for her occupation.

He had talked in his sleep and recounted that he had driven her to her parking garage and parked until she driven away. She knew he had followed her, staying a safe distance behind her so he would not be seen, and had followed her out of town to the barn that served as her storage facility. He had parked behind a tree a few hundred yards behind the building and waited until she returned to her car and drove away. When she was out of sight he returned to the barn, picked the lock on the door, and entered.

He had been shocked at what he saw. A collection of computer equipment, firearms, bullet cartridges, a file drawer with financial records, makeup kits, false noses, contact lenses, wigs, fake moles and beauty marks, a file with the names and phone numbers of plastic surgeons, maps, a "weight suit" that could be worn under clothes to add weight to a person, and ten passports were stacked on and around a desk.

He had read her passports, which were issued for American, British, French, Italian, and Spanish citizens, were all in different names, and listed with different weights and pictures. Georgia Reynolds, Tina Denver, Jacki Olson, Isidora Rozzilli, Livie Callis, Caro Rano, and Eva Bottcher were some of the false identities.

He had sat down in the chair by the desk and said, "Who is Linda Westmorland? What does she want with me? Am I in danger from this woman who says she loves me?"

Susana knew that, as much as she did not want to do so, she had reached a point where she had to leave in order not to be reported to the police. She had left a note for Harold that had mentioned her plans.

It read, "Harold, I love you. We have grown so close over the last few weeks. You are the man with whom I want to spend the rest of my life. I want to have children with you and build a family. I have loved you since I first saw you. You were so kind and polite on the plane. You have always respected me. I have been ordered to go to Rome, Italy by my office to work with a client who has a problem. I do not know how long I will be required to be there. I will be in touch soon."

She knew that they loved each other, but the situation was now one of self-preservation. She had then flown to Amsterdam to perform a contract hit for an abused spouse on a rich, unfaithful, cheating husband and businessman. When she returned to the Dominican Republic she had tailed Harold and his new lover, Juliana Callejas.

When the Sicilian soldier and hitman Baldovino Gioele of the Duante crime family had entered Harold's room to eliminate him, she had shot both Gioele and Callejas.

After Harold had returned home to Gibson City, Susana had called him. She remembered their conversation.

"Harold, this is Susana. You also know me as Linda. We spent wonderful weeks together in the Dominican Republic. We are perfectly matched Harold. We are destined to be together. I know that you loved me as Linda. I can be whoever and whatever you want me to be. We can have a wonderful life together."

She continued, "You have figured out that I killed Juliana. She needed to go. She could have never made you as happy as I can, as Linda, or myself. You belong to me Harold Gatewood, and you are never going to get away. You are, and will be, mine forever."

Gatewood listened but did not speak.

Susana said, "I love you Harold. Please love me."

Harold had not answered, and had hung up the phone. Unknown to Susana he had decided what he must do.

Chapter 10
The ANNM

March 15

IT LOOKED LIKE IT WOULD BE EARLY SPRING in Central Illinois as the weather had broken, the sun had started to shine more each day, and the robins were stating to be seen looking for worms in the yards. If a typical April first snowstorm could be avoided Gatewood would soon be riding his lawn mower around, declaring war on the grass in his yard that would grow unchecked until the first killing frost around Halloween day.

He was still working out each day. His has increased his running program, adding more distance for endurance. His meditation, tai chi, taekwondo, and Brazilian jiu-jitsu exercises were being performed each day. He had also continued to drive to Bloomington for his acupuncture treatments on his arm and shoulder.

He was doing his light weightlifting regime, his agility drills, and watching past and present videos of his swing each day in an attempt to make sure he was using what had made him successful. Also, he was murdering the ball in his hitting drills off the pitching machine and the batting tees. He felt great and knew he was rounding into top hitting shape.

Despite this progress, he had not heard from any baseball team, at any level, in professional baseball about making a comeback. He had instructed his agent, Randle Quinn, to keep him advised about any teams expressing interest, but he had heard nothing. He felt like he was all dressed up, with no place to go.

Harold finished his workout and walked to his house, dodging the small piles of snow placed intermittently around the lawn. He entered the kitchen, poured himself a glass of cold water from the pitcher in the refrigerator, and started the walk toward his favorite chair by the window in the family room. He did not make it there, as the phone rang. He stopped, saw the familiar number on the caller id, and spoke.

"Randle, how are you today? I was just thinking about you."

"Great minds think alike Harold."

"What do you have this morning?"

"Are you in shape?"
"Yes. I have been working out regularly. I feel great."
"I got a call today about a possible option for you."
"Was it from the big leagues?"
"No."
"Overseas? In the Asian leagues?"
"No."
"The Central Illinois Magicians?"
"No."
"Who then Randle?"
"The ANNM."
"The ANNM?"
"Yes."
"What is the ANNM?"
"It is a brand new league being formed in Arizona, New Mexico, and Mexico."
"With teams in America and Mexico?"
"Yes."
"I never heard of it."
"It is a new venture with teams in two countries."
"What classification is it?"
"It is a low A-level competition league."
"What about the players?"
"There will be lots of young kids out of college and high school, and guys who played a year or two and were released."
"How many teams?"
"Six teams each in two divisions. The East division has the Stratton Ravens, Carlin Capitols, Robbins Renegades, Malta Mashers, La Fries Finches, Saulk City Senators, and the Denton Desperadoes. The West division has the Montgomery Mule Deer, South Crosse Commodores, Dobbsville Dukes, Fowler Finches, Hayward Hummingbirds, and Waterford Warriors."
Harold laughed and said, "Hayward Hummingbirds?"
Quinn snickered and said, "Don't laugh Harold. That is the team that wants you."
"Where is Hayward?"
"It is twenty miles South of Tucson, Arizona."
"Who is the skipper?"
"Your old Asian baseball teammate, Scott Binder."
"What do they want me to do?"
"They want you to be their designated hitter."
"Do they really want me to play or is this just a publicity stunt?"

"Obviously they want you to be a draw to boost attendance. But, Scott Binder wants you to play. He hopes you can still hit."

"That sounds fair enough."

"How many teams are in Mexico?"

"Three, all in the Eastern division. They are the Las Fries Finches, Saulk Valley Senators, and Denton Desperadoes."

"What kind of money?"

"It is terrible Harold. It is the minor league minimum."

"How many games?"

"One hundred. The season starts May first and goes to September first."

"What are the playing conditions?"

"The ballfields are new, but they are not like the big leagues. The weather is hot, very hot, because you are in the desert. You will play night games most of the time, when the sun goes down and the temperature drops. I don't know about the quality of the lights. I am sure they are not big league level quality."

"What about the travel?"

"It is a bus league Harold. The distance from the West side teams to the East side teams in the league is far. The road trips are very long, usually a couple weeks."

"How did they hear about me Randle?"

"Scott Binder recommended you because he had heard from Pat Sullivan that you wanted to play again."

"Pat is managing in Phoenix, right?"

"Yes."

"Randle is this the only option out there for me?"

"Harold, I have called everywhere. Everyone thinks you have retired, or are washed up because of your injuries. Unless something would turn up out of the blue, I think this is the only option you have now."

"What do you think Randle?"

"If you really want to play baseball again Harold, this may be your only chance. It is your only option now."

"I understand."

"Harold, it will be scouted. If you can produce you will still get a look. And, Pat Sullivan is just up the road in Phoenix."

"I would enjoy playing for Scott Binder. And, you do have a good point. If I can come back Pat Sullivan would know."

"Harold, Scott talked to Pat. They are rooting for you. If you are ever ready again to play in the big leagues you would have two guys who could help you make it happen."

"Yes, that would be an advantage. When would they want me to report?"

"They will have drills starting on April fifteenth and open on May first. What do you think Harold?"

"Tell them I am going to be a Hummingbird and that I will give them everything I have."

"That is great Harold. I know you want to try again. I will be rooting for you. Give it your best shot."

"I will. Please tell them I will be there on my own around April first. Tell them that I feel great and that I have been working out regularly. I want to get there and acclimate myself to the hot weather. Scott Binder knows how I prepare for the season. Please tell him I will be ready to go."

"Wonderful Harold. Good luck."

"Thanks for everything Randle."

Gatewood clicked off his phone, called his parents in Ft. Myers, Florida to tell them the news, and showered. He then drove to his parent house, took care of their mail, and took care of all farm business that needed to be handled before his parents returned home from Florida. He then returned to his house and started packing.

After completing most of what he needed to do for his trip to Arizona, he sat down in his chair by the window, looked out at his friends the birds and the squirrels and said, "Take care of things here. I will be back in a few months." He then smiled and made himself a promise. "I will make it back to the big leagues. This is my first step."

Chapter 11

The Same Alley

March 16

BAYARDO RAMOS WAS A LOYAL, DEDICATED member of the Masas cartel in Mexico. He respected he cartel's leader Salvador Masas, the El Avispon Picante, the Stinging Hornet. Ramos had performed well for his employers and had just been granted a raise for his successful series of killings of cartel-identified enemies.

The raise had been appreciated as his wife and two young children always needed to be clothed and fed. He loved his family and his family life was much different that his work life in the drug industry, where death was an everyday occurrence. Bayardo made special plans each day that he was the contributor of the murderous violence, and not its recipient.

The cartel had stuck by him and had aided his career development and had schooled him in the fine art of murder. He had learned how to strangle, shoot, poison, torture, and kill his victims in many different types of situations. He was a true professional who loved his work.

Even when he had killed Seve Padilla, a Sargent in the Mexican Drug Control branch of the government, in error, the cartel had stood by him. When Salvador Masas heard the news of Ramos' killing of Padilla he had paused to think about the message it would send to the Mexican military. He was pleased that Ramos had shown the initiative to keep the military in line and protect the cartels interests.

But, Masas was also disturbed with the possible ruffled feathers, and potential crackdown on the cartel's production activities. He decided to make a phone call to smooth over the possible negative impacts of the situation. A quick payment to the then-president of Mexico, Alto Roble smoothed over the problem. The cartel had then instructed Ramos to try to cooperate with the Mexican drug agency in the future.

Ramos paused to remember the details of the incident.

Seve Padilla, a Sargent in the Mexican Drug Contol Division, had watched as his person of interest entered the grocery store. Padilla had exited his military vehicle, walked to the front entry door of the store, and patiently waited. His target, Bayardo Ramos, then walked into the Mexican sunlight carrying a small bag of groceries for his dinner.

Padilla had stuck his pistol into Ramos's back and said, "Walk to the alley with me."

Once the two men were in the alley Padilla had ordered Ramos to put down the bag of groceries, turn and face the building, and put his hands against the wall. Ramos had done as ordered and then spoke, "I have the money for you Sargent Padilla."

"You better have it Ramos or I will blow your head off right here. Give it to me."

Ramos had said that the money was in his pocket and he needed to get it out, to which Padilla agreed. Ramos then reached into the front right pocket of his black slacks, and then, without warning, raised his right leg violently into Padilla's crotch. Padilla had doubled over in pain, dropping his pistol to the street as he yelled in pain.

Ramos had quickly used both hands to grab Padilla behind the head and pulled it downward toward his right thigh that was streaming upward toward Padilla's face. The thigh and head met in a violent crash, sending blood flying from Padilla's nose in all directions. Before the blood droplets could hit the dirt in the alley Ramos followed up with a left hook to the victim's face.

As Padilla reeled backward, exposing his face to his attacker, Ramos had crashed his right fist into the victim's throat. Padilla fell onto the dirt in the alley, grasping for breath. Quickly, Ramos had jumped on top of him and pummeled the victim's face with powerful right and left blows of his massive fists. Padilla was defenseless and was descending into a state of unconsciousness.

Ramos then grabbed Padilla by the front of his uniform shirt and said, "You won't get the money. But I do have something for you before you pass into eternity." Ramos then pulled his nine-inch switchblade knife from his front pocket and violently slit Padilla's throat. Again, blood spurted from the victim, some of it landing on Ramos's black and white-striped shirt, and the massive gold chain around his neck.

Ramos had then wiped his knife on Padilla's shirt, the blood smearing swirls on the khaki-colored uniform top. He then shouted parting comments of "I will keep the money. I earned it more than you did. You and your military men make me do the killing and then you come around for the money like a vulture circling its prey."

Ramos had moved up in the Salvador Masas drug cartel quickly. He had served as a halcone, a falcon, in the organization. He was efficient in his job and kept his superiors informed of the actions of the police, military, and members of rival gangs in his assigned area. Due to his performance and loyalty he had moved into his present position as a sicarios, commonly known as a hitman and enforcer.

His special skills existed in assassination, kidnapping, theft, extortion, protection of the cartel's plaza, or turf, from competing cartels and the military, and a creative array of killing skills. He loved his work as it had offered him a way out of the poverty he had endured as a child, and offered him a chance to become a cult hero that would be honored in narco-corrido, narco-ballads, songs.

He knew his skill set, and dreamed of becoming a lugarteniente, a lieutenant, in the cartel. If he could reach that level he would supervise and control the activities of the halcones and sicarios in his assigned area.

Reaching the level of a capo, a drug lord, was not in his future, as he knew he lacked the intelligence and skills required to assess and appoint the right leaders in the various cartel areas, create alliances with the competing cartel leaders, the military, and the police, and to plan intricate, high-level executions designed to send messages to outside forces that wanted to put the cartel out of business. He was happy where he was, where his skills could be utilized, appreciated, and rewarded.

Today, Ramos had been assigned to shadow another drug control officer who had been shaking down cartel operatives for bribe money. Salvador Masas did not take kindly to people stealing his money, even if they were in the drug control division. He did not mind paying bribe money to the officers in the drug unit but he did draw the line when the same officers became greedy and infringed on his organizations net profits.

Ramos had been ordered to send a message to the Mexican police that greed above the agreed-upon kickback level would not be tolerated. Blood of the victim would send the message with an exclamation point. The hitman followed his subject into the same alley where he had killed Seve Padilla.

His subject, plus three of his fellow-officers were waiting with guns drawn, were in the alley. Ramos went for his pistol but he was too late. The four drug control unit officers filled the air with bullets, headed for Ramos's body. Over twenty bullets tore through the body. He shook in convulsions as the bullets found bone, tissue, and organs as they tore into his torso.

Blood and tissue flew through the air, landing on the germ-filled dirt in the alley. Ramos struggled for his breath, his heart pumped its final beats, and soon he was dead. He was now another victim of the drug problem that infested Mexico at every level of its society. Salvador Maas had not pulled the triggers that killed Ramos. But, he was responsible as his cartel had caused another death.

Chapter 12

The Trip North

March 17

ST. PATRICK'S DAY WAS AN EVENTFUL DAY for many people in the world. For Rosendo and Delfina Tadeo of Venezuela, it was not a day of joy. Their life had descended into poverty, misery, pain, and hopelessness. Their lives in Guatemala had been destroyed when a flood wiped out their farm crops and sent the rich topsoil down the river.

The millions of gallons of water that had flowed down from the mountains to their land outside their village had also taken the couple's dreams with them. They were penniless, and without any way to rebuild their lives. They made a decision. They would immigrate to America, where they could prosper and have a family.

They left on foot, walking down the mountain trails to the valley floor, and started their journey to a new life. Rosendo was twenty-eight years old, five-foot- seven-inches tall, weighed one hundred-three pounds, had dark hair and eyes, and had gone through the sixth grade in school.

He had worked in the fields since he was a boy, and had finally saved enough money to buy a small parcel of land and build a home on it. He was a strong, but unskilled worker.

Delfina had also gone through the sixth grade. She had married Rosendo at a very early age and had helped with the farm work in the fields until she learned she was pregnant. She was now three months along in her nine-month journey to motherhood. She was a pretty girl, twenty-eight years old, dark haired, had dark-brown eyes, and was petite in stature.

Conditions were terrible in Venezuela, and she had been selling her hair to help earn money for the family. There was no economic activity, no jobs, and no income. The political problems in the country were massive, as the Nazoa government was corrupt, involved in the drug trade through Mexico, and had been teetering on the brink of collapse for months.

The couple had decided to join the hordes of people heading through the Central America into Mexico and making their way into the Southwestern states of America. They would join people from El Salvador, Guatemala, Honduras, Nicaragua, Costa Rica, Belize, and Panama on the road to a better life.

They would face dire conditions, sickness, starvation, robbery, kidnapping, extortion, gang violence, sexual assault, and the harsh elements of the desert if they illegally made it across the American border. They would have to enter America by using their own wits as they had no money to pay a Mexican coyote to escort them into the promised land.

If they made it to America they would face deportation as they would be illegal immigrants under American law. If they managed to stay in the country they would have trouble adjusting to American culture as they could not speak English. They would perhaps be forced to turn to crime to support themselves, as many illegals would do. Plus, they loved Venezuela and would always be loyal to their country of birth.

Their journey through Venezuela, Columba, Panama, Costa Rica, Nicaragua, Honduras, and into Guatemala had taken five months. They had walked, and gone from migrant camp to migrant camp. Delfina was now getting closer to her delivery due date and walking was becoming difficult.

They hoped they could cross into America and have the baby there as their "anchor baby" would be a citizen and their chances of not being deported would improve based on that fact. Delfina's condition now made the long trek through Mexico an across the desert in America close to impossible. They needed to find another pathway across the border.

Rosendo learned that many people were now using the railroads that ran from Guatemala to Mexico to speed up their journey. That choice was not without danger, as they could be accosted by gangs, beaten, robbed, and thrown off the train. Despite the risks, the couple decided to take the trains to Mexico.

They learned which trains were heading North, and boarded one late in the evening. They found refuge in an empty railroad car and rode for a day and a half toward Mexico. They were awakened when the train stopped in a small city and a gang of twelve men hopped into the empty railroad car.

In a few short hours, Resendo had been beaten and robbed of the couple's last finances. Delfina had been raped and beaten. The Tadeos were then thrown off the train. After spending a day to recover, they tried to board the next train North, hoping for better fortune.

The couple hid in the train yard and waited for the train to stop, then moved quietly toward the back of the long line of cars. No open cars were available. Resndo saw a lineman heading toward them, to make sure the cars were still safely connected.

He told Delfina to move to the end of the last car of the train and wait for his signal to join him once he had evaded the lineman and found a way to board the train. She hid and waited patiently for his signal. She did not notice the train behind her backing up to couple the car she was hiding behind to the rest of the train.

As she concentrated on what might take place in front of her, the train behind her moved closer and closer, with the end car's coupler jaws spread, ready to connect with the car Delfina was hiding behind.

The coupler of the approaching train car slammed into her body, smashing it into the coupler jaws of the railcar she was hiding behind. Her body was squashed between the couplers. She was still alive. Rosendo had heard her scream and had run to her aid. He was joined by the lineman who called the railyard office and requested medical help.

Delfina was dying. If the cars were moved her body would be torn in two pieces when the jaws of the knuckle-style couplers separated, causing her and her baby's insides to be pulled apart, causing instant death. The accident was one that happened in many railroad yard accidents for years.

A priest was called to administer the last rites. Delfina was allowed to say goodbye to Resendo. She cried, kissed him goodbye, and the train backed up, separating the cars and Delfina and her unborn baby's insides. It was a hideous sight.

Resendo was taken to a hospital as he was in shock. He stayed for three days, and was released. He decided to continue on his journey to America, as that is what Delfina would have wanted him to do. He traveled zombie-like for five days on top of the train cars, hiding out when the freight trains would stop in the stations.

He stayed on the trains until they reached the main city that straddled the Mexican and Mexican border. He hid out for three days, watching the coyotes lead illegal immigrants over the border at night, and trying to figure out a plan to safely cross the border on his own.

He saw an opening on the fourth night and climbed the border fence, dropped to the other side, and ran up the hill. He was in America now. He walked through the desert for two days, becoming dehydrated and weak.

He pushed on. He was only eight miles from Hayward, Arizona, and twenty-eight miles from Tucson. He was tired. He decided he could not go on without sleep. He laid down after the brutally hot sun dipped below the horizon. The night became cold and Resendo shivered with the chills.

When the sun rose he next day, and the temperatures climbed to over one hundred and five degrees, Resendo tried to go on. He dropped to the ground in the desert, his face pressed against the hot sand. He imagined he saw Delfina walking toward him holding their new baby, a boy who was now an "anchor baby" and an American citizen. He smiled, exhaled, and passed into the grips of death.

Resendo and Defino Taedeo, and their unborn son, were now three more victims of the problems in Venezuela, Mexico, and the march of illegal immigrants toward America.

Chapter 13

A Sailor

March 18

HE WAS CALLED CHICO MARINERO, which meant sailor boy. No one, not even he, knew his real name. He had been born in San Armando, Mexico. His home was on the Western side of Baja California. In truth his home was the sea. His father had been a fisherman and from the time Chico could walk he would accompany his father in the boat as he fished for the family's meals and income.

He loved the sea, its fishes and creatures, and the solitude it brought him. He felt lost when he was not in the boat on the seas or oceans. He would venture out early when he became competent enough to navigate the seas himself. Often times he would spend several days on the water.

He knew the shipping routes, and currents from San Armando to San Diego, California as well as any man alive. When people would ask him if he were married he would say, "Yes, to the seas and oceans."

He had joined the Mexican navy when he became older, serving in the submarine fleet. As much as he loved being on the seas and oceans, he loved being under them more. Being a submarine sailor was his passion, and his calling.

He did not suffer from the conditions that made many sailors unfit for submarine duty. He did not suffer from claustrophobia. In fact he loved being confined in a submarine and considered the small space his own.

He was not bothered by the confinement or the possibility of not having enough air to breathe in the submarine. His air was his own and he would not worry about getting anyone else's.

When he retired from the Mexican navy he returned to San Armando to be near the sea. He fished in his own boat but still yearned for the chance to travel the seas in his own submarine. Plus, he wanted to make more money to make his life more comfortable.

He had been approached by the Salvador Masas cartel to serve in the cartel's submarine fleet and run drugs from Baja California to the areas off

Catalina Island. The drugs would be offloaded from the submarine to a speed boat while at sea.

The speed boat would then deliver the drugs to an area above Los Angeles where they would be offloaded and sent to safe houses for later sale and distribution to the street junkies.

The profits from a load of cocaine and heroin from a narco-submarine were massive, stretching into the hundreds of millions of dollars, depending on the size of the sub. Chico was a well-paid, competent skipper of his own submarine who always made his deliveries.

He had never lost a shipment or had to have his sub sunk due to being caught by the American Coast Guard. He was the "Stinging Hornet's" favorite skipper.

Narco-subs were usually constructed of fiberglass, eighteen to twenty-five feet in length, and typically carried loads of ten to fifteen tons of drugs. Cost for a sub was miniscule compared to the profits of the cargo. A typical sub would cost several million dollars to construct but the payoff could be up to several hundred times its cost.

In order to prevent detection from aerial surveillance planes the subs were painted blue to blend in with the ocean's water color. Subs could hold four crew members in a cramped cockpit area. No head, the restroom, was on the sub. Every inch of room was packed with drugs.

The sub had ballast tanks that could be open to allow water to enter and gain weight in order to ride low in the water, which would help prevent detection. Satellite navigation electronics were standard equipment. Chico was also skilled with the sextant, the tool used by ancient seafarers to plot their course.

Diesel engines powered the subs and permitted speeds up to eighteen knots, or over twenty-four miles an hour. A cooling system allowed the exhaust of the engines to be piped under the water along the bottom of the ship which helped prevent the sub being detected by infrared systems, or sonar or radar. The subs ran just under the surface of the water and created no wake.

The subs were used one time, and then sunk after a successful unloading of the cargo. If they were detected and in danger of being caught by the Coast Guard the sub, cargo and all, would be sunk before being captured.

Chico was the superstar of the cartel fleet and always traveled alone as he loved the solitude of the sea. His latest mission was a delivery of cocaine up the Baja coast to an area West of Catalina Island. Chico had made good time, as the seas had been quiet since his departure. He had been escorted by a pod of orcas during the first third of his trip. He was joined by migrating humpback whales for the rest of his journey.

Whales, dolphins, and sharks were constant companions during his trips and he had grown to love their company. He considered them his close friends as he had more in common with them than he had with most people.

Ten miles from his destination he was spotted by a American Coast Guard vessel. The chase was on. Chico changed course several times and tried to get out of the open seas in order to prevent further detection. He steered into nearby shore channels as best as he could but he would not shake the Coast Guard ship.

He took it as a point of pride that he had not ever been captured or lost a ship's cargo but he was now concerned that he would soon be caught, and his record would soon be blemished.

He sensed the Coast Guard vessel was close to him but he dared not let the water out of the ballast tanks in fear that he would not be able to submerge again. Against his better judgement, he decided that he needed to surface in order check out the American ship. When he surfaced he was shocked to see the Coast Guard cutter heading straight toward him, at top speed.

He steered the sub to the starboard, right, side as best as he could. But, it was not enough. The approaching ship rammed his sub broadside at forty knots, forty-six miles an hour. Chico was killed instantly, and millions of dollars of drug profits sank to the bottom of Davey Jones locker.

When news of Chico's death reached the "Stinging Hornet", he sat speechless in his chair. It was another death related to his cartel's actions. He looked as if he had lost the only friend he had in the world. The sad part was that he actually had.

Chapter 14

Addiction

March 19

SINCE AGREEING TO JOIN THE HAYWOOD HUMMINGBIRDS, Harold Gatewood had worked out feverishly as he would soon be heading to Arizona to start his comeback. He packed the night before, was up early, and left at five a.m. His plans were to drive as far as Coffeyville, Kansas.

Two hundred and forty miles into the trip he listened to the news on the radio. A thirty-two year old former college professor and author with a masters' degree in early childhood behavior named Stephanie Walters had died of a cocaine and heroin overdose in a suburb of Tucson, Arizona.

She had been an attractive, blue-eyed blonde, five-foot-eight-inches tall, and was a former beauty queen from Arizona. She had weighed one hundred thirty-five pounds, had been married for eight years until she was sued for divorce by her former husband for having numerous affairs.

She had lost her job due to her addiction problem, then had lost her money as she had used her financial settlement to fuel her addiction. She had lost custody of her three children, and had been to drug rehab two separate times, each one ending in an unsuccessful attempt to kick her habit.

Having nowhere to live, she migrated to the street, became a prostitute, and suffered severe weight loss. Her eyes were sunken into their sockets when she had died, and her teeth had rotted down to her gums. She had lost her money, beauty, and life to drugs.

She had progressed to heroin, and had the track marks to prove she had been a professional junkie. Reports confirmed that her drugs had come from Columbia, to Central America, the Mexico, and finally across the Southwestern border of America to the streets of the Phoenix area.

The supplier of the drugs from Mexico was the Salvador Masas cartel, the most famous and notorious cartel leader in Mexico. He was known as El Avispon Picante, "the Stinging Hornet."

Stephanie's parents had confirmed that she had shown the symptoms of cocaine addiction for several years. She had suffered from withdrawal he numerous times she had tried to kick her habit. She had enjoyed he euphoria and high energy the drug provided, which fueled her desire for more of the product.

She suffered from mood swings, paranoia, insomnia, psychotic episodes, high blood pressure, rapid heartbeat, panic attacks, cognitive impairments, and personality changes.

She would also suffer from dysphoria, mood swings, depression, anxiety, psychological and physical weakness, various pains, and compulsive cravings.

When she was using she was happy, energetic, and talkative. When she was not she went into a manic condition similar to schizophrenia. She would become aggressive, paranoid, restless, confused, hallucinate, itch herself constantly, and think about suicide. Her nose ran nonstop, and her appearance was always pale and unhealthy.

Besides two stints in rehab, she had tried the Cocaine Anonymous twelve-step program, cognitive behavioral therapy, acupuncture, and hypnosis, all to no avail. Medically, she had tried the whole pharmacy inventory, including anticonvulsants, narcolepsy drugs, and all of the quack, unapproved drugs rumored to help an addict.

She suffered cardiovascular disease and brain damage where the blood vessels contracted in her brain, which had caused several strokes. Mercifully, her heart and kidneys shut down and she was released from her demons, cocaine and heroin. She passed into death, peaceful at last.

The newscaster finished the report by saying, "She died as a result of the Salvador Masas cartel drug smuggling operation into Arizona. Even though he did not pull force the drugs into her body, he is still responsible for her death. We good citizens of Arizona demand that something be done to stop the cartel's influence in our state."

Gatewood drove on in silence, thinking about two people he knew had died of drug problems, his Tokyo Cardinal teammate Mario Kennedy, and his former lover, crime princess Kimiko Michi Hayato.

Harold and his road roommate Scott Binder, had been eye-witnesses to the tragedy. He remembered the event as he drove. Scott Binder had said, "Are you hungry Harold?"

"Yes, let's get out of here and go for a snack."

The roommates walked down the street to a restaurant for their snack, then headed back to the hotel, where a small group of people were gathered, looking up at a ninth-floor balcony. A man was standing on his patio ledge, yelling disjointed phrases at the sky. The man had locked his room door, and had been conducting classes in self-pity and irrationality from the patio ledge for ten minutes. The closer Harold and Scott looked at the daredevil above, the more they realized the man's face, withdrawn and tortured from the effects of cocaine addiction, belonged to Mario Kennedy.

The two ballplayers ran to the lobby desk, told a lie that they were the roommates and friends of the man on the ledge, and grabbed a second room key from the desk employee. Soon, they were at the room door, which they opened. They then inched toward Mario Kennedy, and the patio, in an attempt to talk him down from the ledge.

"Mario, this is Harold and Scott."
"Stay away."
"How are you Mario?"
"I am dead."
"Why are you on the ledge?"
"I am going to jump and make my death official."
"Don't do that."
"Why not?"
"Because you have a lot to live for, you have things to do yet."
"No I don't. My life is ruined. I have made a terrible mess of my life."
"You can correct all that Mario."
"No. My career is over."
"What do you mean? You are pitching great."
"No, not that. I have been busted."
"How?"
"I failed my drug test."
"You can get clean, by going to rehab, and then come back."
"No. I have a history of drug use already. No one will ever take a chance on me again."
"Mario, there is life after baseball."
"No there isn't. I can't do anything else."
"Sure you can."
"No. I won't go back to my hometown to work at the lumberyard."
"Mario, please get down from there."
"No."

Gatewood pleaded, "Please get down Mario. Scott and I are going to take your hands and help you down, to safety. Mario, you know I am afraid of heights, and will be scared to death out there. Please get down."

"No. I am going to do it."
"Don't do it."
"The Yakuza are after me. The Yamaguchi Shifu family, and that crazy daughter of Daisuke Hayato got me hooked on cocaine."
"Kimiko Hayato?"

"Yes, she is as crazy as it gets. I should know because I am crazy now too, all because of her."

"Mario, we can help you."

"Gatewood, I never liked you. Shut up!"

"Get down Mario."

"What do you know Gatewood? You are her boyfriend so you may be next."

"Get down."

"No. Goodbye boys. I can fly like a bird."

Kennedy lurched from the ledge, and headed to a crashing death on the sidewalk below. Harold and Scott had made it to the ledge just as Mario jumped, and saw his body, arms and legs flailing, land with a sickening thud below, sending blood in a three-hundred-sixty degree explosion pattern. Harold turned his head, trying not to throw up, then inched back to the safety of the room. Scott Binder fared no better, as he shook uncontrollably for five minutes, after witnessing the most gruesome event of his life.

Gatewood cringed at the memory, and drove on toward Coffeyville. His thoughts then turned to Kimiko Michi Hyato's struggle with the drugs her family pushed.

Harold's thoughts of the event came rushing back to him.

A knock on his apartment door brought Harold back to reality. Looking out the peephole of the door, he saw a medium height, slender, bespectacled, Japanese man wearing a hat, and peering back at him through the peephole.

"How can I help you?"

"Mr. Harold Gatewood?"

"Yes."

"I am Kenta Yoshirou, Tokyo Police Chief."

"Please let me see your badge."

"Here it is."

"Okay. How can I help you?"

"There has been an incident Mr. Gatewood."

"What is it?"

"It relates to your girlfriend, Kimiko Hayato."

"Wait a minute. I will unlock the door."

"Thank you."

"What has happened?"

"She is in bad shape, a drug overdose."

"Oh no."

"When did you last see her?"

"Yesterday morning. We had a night game on the road."

"Where did you see her?"

"We were together at the hotel."
"What was the purpose of her visit?"
"We have been dating. She surprised me, nude in my bed."
"How long did she stay?"
"I did not see her after the visit in the morning so I do not know."
"Was there a romantic purpose of her visit?"
"Only on her part. I told her I could not see her anymore."
"How did she react?"
"She became hysterical. I asked her to leave as I was afraid she would harm herself if she stayed."
"So she left right away?"
"We talked for about thirty minutes, then I sent her away."
"When was that?"
"It was mid-morning."
"What was her condition when she left?"
"She had calmed a bit, but she was still upset."
"Where did she go?"
"I don't know."
"Did you see her again?"
"No."
"Okay."
"Is she alive?"
"Barely, she is in the hospital. She is close to death."
"Will she survive?"
"That is a question for her doctors."
"If she survives, what will happen to her?"
"She will probably be put in rehab, or the insane asylum."
"How long?"
"I have no idea."
"This is horrible."
"Did you two love each other?"
"She loved me but I knew it would not work. I did not really love her."
"Are you familiar with her background?"
"Yes."
"Have you met her father?"
"No."
"My advice is to be cautious, as he is a very powerful man."
"Thank you."
"The Yamaguchi Shifu crime family always settles their scores."
"Thanks for the warning."
"Do you have a bodyguard? If not, you should consider getting one."

"Okay."

"Is there anything I can do for you Mr. Gatewood?"

"Yes."

"What?"

"Can you please tell me what hospital she is in right now?"

"Yes, come to the window with me. Do you see the tallest building over there?"

"Yes."

"That is it."

"Thank you."

"One other thing officer, was there was a suicide note? If there was, what did it say?"

"It said that she loved you very much, and did not want to live without you. Do you really understand the danger you are now in Mr. Gatewood?"

"Yes."

"You need to understand that this is the Yamaguchi Shifu's second-in-command, and the daughter of their leader, and they will hold you responsible for her suicide attempt."

"I did not cause this to happen."

"They will not see it that way."

"I understand."

"Get that bodyguard if you want to keep living."

"Okay."

Harold was shaken by the conversation with the Tokyo police chief, and needed to think about what he should do concerning Kimiko's situation. He wanted to see her, and to see her doctor to find out the possibility of her survival. He walked the two blocks to the hospital, thinking about Kimiko's condition, and what to ask her doctor about the situation.

"Hi, can you tell me about the condition of a patient, Kimiko Hayato?"

"Are you a family member?"

"No."

"I can only give information to family members."

"We were dating. Please tell me her condition."

"I should not do this, but I will. She is under sedation."

"How bad is she?"

"She is fighting for her life."

"The police told me she tried to commit suicide. Who found her?"

"Her mother. She had stopped by to see her, found her passed out on the floor, and then she called for help."

"Can I talk to her doctor?"

"No. I am sorry."

"Thank you for your help. Can I call later to check on her condition?"

"Yes, but you should ask for me, Linda, as I know your relationship to Kimiko."

The trip to the hospital had uncovered no new information about Kimiko's chances of survival, but it had helped Harold to some degree, as he had shown his concern for his ex-girlfriend. On the way out of the front door, an older Japanese lady, concern and stress visible on her face, stopped Harold and spoke to him. She was Kimiko's mother.

"Mr. Gatewood?"

"Yes."

"I am Kimiko's mother."

"Hello. I am sorry about Kimiko."

"Thank you for coming to see her."

"Of course. I am so upset. How is she?"

"Very bad."

Harold asked, "What do the doctors say about her recovery?"

"The say the next twenty four hours are critical."

"I am praying for her."

"Thank you. You know that she loved you very much."

"Yes. We had a close friendship."

"We appreciate your concern for Kimiko."

"I care about her recovery."

The conversation between Kimiko's mother and Harold was interrupted by a man, obviously distraught and angry, who demanded that the woman, Kimiko's mother, return to her seat in the hospital waiting room. He then spoke to Gatewood, "Young man, I want to talk with you. I am Kimiko's father, Daisuke Hayato."

"Hello. I am sorry about Kimiko's condition.""

"My wife is more forgiving than I. You are the cause of the problem."

"Sir, I am not."

"Since you have arrived in Japan Kimiko has not been herself."

"I do not understand why you said that."

"She has lost all touch with reality, her work, her family, her culture, and her traditions."

"I am not the cause of that."

"She has fallen in love with you, for all of the wrong reasons."

Harold answered, "She is a wonderful woman, but I never gave her the impression that we would always be together."

"You Americans come here to make money, and then leave. You have no respect for our country, our traditions, or our families. Do not ever come to this hospital again. You have no business here."

"I am only trying to help. Sir, she is my friend, and I want her to get well."
"Stay away !"
"Calm down Sir."
"You have no idea how powerful I am. If you value your life you will stay away."
"If that is how you want it, then I will honor your wishes."
"Leave. If my daughter dies, I will kill you !"

The walk back to his apartment was one marked with dejection and disappointment, due to Kimiko's dire condition, and her father's hate-filled outburst blaming him for suicide attempt. He would be happy to return to the serenity of his apartment, and then to the one place where he could block out the events which had been clouding his life, the ballpark.

Kimiko Hayato had survived her suicide attempt, had stabilized, and had been transferred to a treatment center for rehabilitation related to cocaine addiction, and mental problems.

Her father, Daisuke Hayao, was pleased that his daughter had survived, and had been transferred to a treatment center where she could return to good physical and mental health. His blame for Gatewood as the catalyst for his daughter's condition, and his rage and hatred for him had increased to an unhealthy level.

Harold was jolted back to reality when he nearly ran his car off of the pavement. He steadied the car's path and again thought about the newscaster's words. Yes, Salvador Masas was responsible for Stephanie Walters' death because he had supplied the drugs that had led to her death.

Gatewood then thought about the additional comments the newscaster had made. Harold agreed, something must be done to stop the Masas cartel.

Chapter 15

The Wild, Wild West

March 20

GATEWOOD ARRIVED IN COFFEYVILLE, KANSAS AFTER A FULL DAY OF DRIVING, checked into a motel, and immediately showered, went to bed, and crashed into deep REM sleep. He was up early the next day, chugged down some hot chocolate and oatmeal, and relaxed until eight thirty a.m. He then headed to scene of the disastrous Dalton Gang attempt to rob two banks at the same time.

The Dalton Brothers Gang was comprised of Bob, Grat, Emmet Dalton, Bill Power, and Dick Broadwell. The gang had ridden from Missouri to rob the C.M. Condon and company bank and the First National Bank of Coffeyville.

The robberies failed when they were told they had to wait for the time lock to open the safe at the Condon Bank. The townspeople realized a robbery was in play and armed themselves. When the gang reentered the street bullets flew through the air. When the dust cleared, Bob and Grat Dalton, Bill Power, and Dick Broadwell had been killed and Emmet Dalton had been wounded twenty-three times.

Gatewood then visited the Coffeyville town museum and read about one of the greatest pitchers ever to play big league baseball, Coffeyville native Walter "Big Train" Johnson. After finishing his visit at the museum he drove to the cemetery plots of all four gang members who were killed. He then headed out of town toward his next wild, wild-west stop, Clayton, New Mexico.

In Clayton, Gatewood visited Tom, "Black Jack", Ketchum's gravesite. Ketchum was a notorious thief and killer. It was rumored that he once shot a man for snoring. Ketchum met the hangman's noose in Clayton. Unfortunately for "Black Jack" he was decapitated when the noose was strung too tight around his neck.

Gatewood then drove to Raton, New Mexico and fished in a reservoir where the New Mexico record Norther Pike had been caught. He managed to catch a nice fourteen pounder in shallow water. He finished off the day by going to Cimarron to spend the night at the famous Regis Hotel, which was reported to be haunted.

Many famous Old Western celebrities had stayed at the hotel including Wyatt and Morgan Earp of Gunfight at the O.K. Corral in Tombstone fame, Jesse James, Buffalo Bill Cody, Sherriff Pat Garrett who killed Billy the Kid, gunfighter Clay Allison, world-famous artist Fredrick Remington, General Lew Wallace, who became he author of the novel "Ben-Hur" and was appointed the territorial governor of New Mexico who had failed to honor the pardon of Billy the Kid, and the infamous "Black Jack Ketchum", before he lost his head.

Ghosts in the hotel were reported to be those of the original owner's wife, Mary lambert, whose perfume could be smelled if she was roaming the hallways at night, and J. H. Wright, who was shot in the back and killed after winning the hotel in a poker game. Gatewood got up in the middle of the night to look for the two ghosts but did not find them.

The next morning Harold headed to Taos, the artist colony, where he stopped to for a lunch break. He then continued on to Manassa, Colorado, the home of legendary world champion boxer Jack Dempsey. He visited the museum that held artifacts of Dempsey's boxing career, and then turned in for the night.

He was up early the next day and drove to Navaho Lake, New Mexico where he spent the next two days fishing for rainbow and brown trout in the San Juan River. He fly fished with a guide for one day and then fished on his own the second day.

He was successful in landing many nice fish in the protected area of the river near the Navajo dam and also in the non-regulated part of the river further away from the dam. His biggest fish was an eight-pound brown trout, a beautiful fish. His largest rainbow trout was a four and one-half pounder taken in the upper river near the dam.

He was enjoying the drive out to Arizona but he was getting itchy to be there so he could start his workouts again. He spent two nights in nearby Farmington, spending the days looking at the Indian history of the Navajo, Jicarilla-Apache, Ute, and Hopi tribes in the area. His next stop was the four corners monument where the stares of New Mexico, Colorado, Arizona, and Utah meet. He stood with a foot or an arm in each of the four states.

As he headed to the Grand Canyon in Northern Arizona, he could not help but shudder about his visit to the Indian areas, as it brought back memories of his bad experiences with another Native American, Susana Richards, from Scalp, Minnesota.

Once he reached the canyon he marveled at the beauty of the biggest hole in the earth he had ever seen. He also watched a mountain lion through his binoculars. He daydreamed as he watched the lion, as he had always planned to harvest one.

He then headed to Winslow, Arizona where he stayed the night. The next morning he posed for a picture, "standing on the corner in Winslow, Arizona", as the famous song had stated. He then headed to Flagstaff where he saw two trophy elk as he drove the road into town. He headed South and descended in elevation as he drove down to Phoenix, where he spent the night.

The next morning he drove South again, through Tucson and into his new home-away-from-home, Hayward, home of the newly created Hayward Hummingbirds of the ANNM professional baseball league. He checked into his apartment that he had rented online before he left Gibson City.

He worked out the next three days and then took a day off to drive to Tombstone, where he visited the site of the famous Gunfight at the O.K. Corral between Wyatt, Morgan, and Virgil Earp and their friend Doc Holliday and the outlaw group of "Cowboys" named Ike and Billy Clanton, Frank and Tom McLaury, and Billy Claiborne.

The short but deadly battle, where thirty shots were fired, lasted only thirty seconds. Billy Clanton, and the McLaury brothers were killed, and Morgan and Virgil Earp, and Doc Holliday were injured. Only mythical hero Wyatt Earp escaped without injury.

Harold then headed to the national forest Southwest of Tombstone and South of Hayward, where many beautiful species could be seen. He hiked for a couple hours, thought about the world famous quail hunting for Mearns, Gambels, and Scaled species in the area, and then headed home to his apartment in Hayward.

On the trip back he thought about the mental notes he had taken about the closeness of the area to the Mexican border, the same border where the Masas cartel funneled drugs into America. He had no idea that this area would soon play an important part in his life for the next several months.

Chapter 16

No Capital Punishment

April 1

GATEWOOD HAD SLEPT SOUNDLY. He cleaned up, ate breakfast and dove into the morning newspaper before starting his workouts for the day. He was startled when he read the headline, which said, "WIFE OF EX-PRESIDENT OF MEXICO PLEADS GUILTY TO MURDER."

Harold was amazed as he read the details of the murder of Alto Roble. Angelica Roble, admitted that she killed her husband in exchange for a plea deal that would make her prison sentence less difficult. She stated that Alto been spending more nights on his yacht, away from the family. Roble was enjoying his drugs from the Salvador Masas. Masas, El Avispon Picante, the stinging hornet, had instructed his cartel to provide as much cocaine as Roble demanded, all free of charge.

The President's appetite for drugs, and the sexual company of his harem of women was now out of control, much to the my displeasure said Angelica Conejo Roble. The first lady, a beautiful woman who had grown up in a rich, privileged family, was a loving wife and devoted mother. She admitted that she had had grown to hate her husband for his philandering, drinking, drug use, and time away from the family. Their marriage was in chaos, and was splitting at the seams.

Angelica testified that she had arranged to have the nanny take the children to a play, and had given the rest of the employees a night off. She was alone in the house. She had dressed in black sweatpants and a black top, tennis shoes, and had packed a small, black-colored gym bag with the items she would need for her appointment later in the evening.

As she drove to her destination, Mrs. Roble had smiled and thought how her mission would be a satisfying one, one which she had spent several years longing to enjoy. She had parked her car at the back of the parking lot, in an area where the security cameras would not see her. She had then walked toward the yacht, hugging the edge of the wall that was also unseen by the security cameras.

When she reached the ramp leading up to her destination she put had on a black face mask, with holes cut out for her eyes and mouth, and surgical gloves to prevent her fingerprints from being left at the scene. She had headed up the stairs and to sleeping quarters. She then quietly opened the door and saw her target, naked on the bed. Next to him were two beautiful women, also naked. All three of the sexual trifecta were out cold from the effects of too much cocaine.

Angelica then removed a small, twenty-two-caliber pistol from her gym bag, walked first to her husband, Alto Roble, the president of Mexico. She nudged him gently, which brought him to a semi-conscious state. As he slipped toward slumber again, she had gently shaken him again and said, "Darling, please look at me."

Alto opened his eyes and slurred out the words, "Angelica, is that you?"

"Yes dear. I have something for you."

"What is it?"

"It is something that will let you forever be with your treasured beauties, like these two young girls next to you."

"Will I like it?"

"Oh yes dear, you will forever enjoy it."

"Will you like it too?"

"Oh darling, I will love it. I have wanted it for you for many years."

Alto, still groggy from his cocaine and sexual orgy had stuttered out the words, "Wonderful honey. When can I have it?"

"Do you really want it Alto?"

"Yes, can I have it soon?"

"Yes."

"Then please give it to me now."

To please him, Angelica then placed her pistol in his hand, helped him lift it to his head, placed a small pillow over the pistol barrel, put his finger on the lever, and helped his index finger pull the trigger. She helped him fire a bullet into his brain, killing him instantly. She immediately checked to see if the muffled sound of the shot had awakened the two naked girls on the bed. They were still asleep.

The girl closest to Alto, her head resting on his stomach, was young, beautiful, and hooked on cocaine. She was just the type her now-deceased husband had preferred. She was from Argentina, had olive-colored skin, a nicely-shaped body, and long dark-brown hair that extended to her mid-back. Angelica then put the gun in her dead husband's hand, placed the small pillow over her pistol's barrel and with a gentle squeeze of her husband's hand, the activated the trigger. The beautiful girl was killed, the bullet entering her temple.

She then moved the second girl, from Cuba, on to the other side of husband's body. The girl was as limp as a rag, still in a cocaine coma. She was a carbon copy of the girl from Argentina. Only the country of her birth, Cuba, was different. Angelica then repeated the same process as she had done with the first girl, using her deceased husband's finger to pull the trigger. The second girl now also laid dead on top of Alto.

Angelica had admired her work, smiled and then finished her plan. She used Alto's hand to pull the trigger, and send three more shots into the bedroom walls, to simulate that he had been in a cocaine-induced rage, and had been firing the gun in many directions. She then placed Alto's hand in his gun, next to his body.

She stepped back from the bed, admired her work, and then walked down the ramp from the yacht, out of sight of security cameras, and to the parking lot where she drove away unseen, and free from any video surveillance. Angelica giggled as she drove off. She was proud of her ability to plan a perfect murder of her worthless, cheating husband.

She then drove home, showered, washed the clothes she had used at the murder scene, and placed them in their proper places in the drawers in her bedroom. She then dressed in her nightgown, and curled up on the couch with a book to await the nanny and the children's return from the play. She had smiled and said, "Now I am free of him forever. I will take the children away from here where they can be safe from his evil lifestyle.

No capital punishment existed in Mexico so Angelica Roble would not face the death penalty. She is expected to receive a sentence of forty years for premeditated, first-degree murder o her husband, and similar sentences or the two women's deahs. She will never be eligible for parole.

Harold put down the newspaper, smiled, and said, "Even that was too good for a rotten human being like Alto Roble."

Chapter 17

The Rodeo

April 1

GATEWOOD PUT IN A SPIRITED WORKOUT AND FINISHED THE DAY with a mile walk in the hot Arizona sunshine. He had been affected by the hot, humid air and was glad to hit the shower when he returned to his apartment. He made plans to eat and then go to the rodeo that was being held in nearby Tucson.

After arriving at the municipal stadium he moved to the box seats closest to the dirt infield and sat down. He watched the groundskeepers smooth out the dirt in the infield area and then struck up a conversation with an older couple who were sitting in the box seats next to him.

He admitted that he had seen only one rodeo, many years ago when he was a kid. The couple was very knowledgeable and explained each event and what each participant should try to accomplish when it was their turn to perform.

Harold asked them how they had become such knowledgeable fans of the rodeo. They mentioned that they followed the professional rodeo circuit because their daughter was a barrel-riding regular participant. They mentioned that she competed in the major competitions worldwide. When Harold asked the couple their daughter's name they replied, "Sarah Belleza."

Harold watched each event and marveled at the skill of both the cowboy and cowgirl participants. In between events he would read his program about the evening's event. When he reached page twenty-one a smile came to his face. Sarah Belleza was featured in the two-page article.

She was not only a world-class barrel rider but she was a world-class knockout, a real beauty. She had dark black hair down to her mid-back, dark-brown bedroom eyes, long eyelashes, a perfectly shaped face, luscious lips, beautiful white teeth, an hourglass-shaped figure, a nice, bountifully-blessed chest, nice legs, and a heart-grabbing smile.

He read the article about her successes on the Women's Professional Rodeo Association tour. Harold learned that she was not only a world-class beauty, but she was also a world-class barrel-riding champion. She had won many events, including the Calgary Stampede title five times.

She consistently scored times close to the world's record in her event, and had stated in the article that she hoped to set a new record soon.

The article described the secret of her success as being a lover of the rodeo and her event. She had grown up in a rodeo family, and learned the sport from her parents who had both competed on the professional circuit.

Barrel racing was one of the five events on the rodeo circuit. Also included were calf roping, team roping, bareback riding, and bull riding.

Harold read on about Sarah's specialty, and realized there was much more to the sport, and the beautiful young woman, than met the eye. She was a college graduate, holding a master's degree in chemistry.

The article described the barrel racing event. The rider would enter the ring at full speed, pass by the electric eye that measured the performance time at the starting line, and progressed in a cloverleaf pattern around three barrels set in a triangle-like shape.

The rider would approach the first barrel while controlling the speed of the horse to make a perfect turn, then proceed to each of the next two barrels, repeating the process. Then a sprint back to the original starting line would give the contestant their time for the ride. He read about the importance of the rider in controlling the horse, sitting back in the saddle when approaching the barrels, and holding their legs close to the horse's side during turns around the barrels.

When it was Sarah's time to perform he watched her parents move up on the edge of their seats and look at the starting line. In a flash, rider and horse were going full speed at the three barrels. The horse and rider moved as one when they navigated around the barrels and sped past the finish line. The time was shown on the scoreboard. It was one-half second off the world record.

After the ride Harold told the couple that he was sure they were very proud of their talented daughter. The couple then asked him what he did for a living. When he told them he was with the Hayward Hummingbirds they asked him if he was the manager. He smiled and said he was a player.

At the end of the rodeo the couple asked Harold if he would like to join them, and their daughter for a snack. Harold jumped at the chance and the group headed to a nearby restaurant.

Sarah Belleza joined them later. As she walked through the door and headed to the table Harold knew that she was special. She smiled when she reached them, kissed her parents and shook Harold's hand when they were introduced. The conversation between the group was very relaxed.

Harold learned that her parents owned a ranch outside of Hayward, about three miles from his apartment. They were lifelong residents of the area, and had built a nice life and close family. Sarah was as pleasant as she was beautiful. She was down-to-earth, just like Harold.

When the group had left the table to leave Sarah stayed back to talk to Harold and to let her parents walk a short distance ahead. The attraction had been mutual, and the two exchanged phone numbers. Over the next two weeks, the ballplayer and he barrel racer spent much time together, and became close. Soon, they were lovers. Harold had learned that Sarah was not only a world-class barrel racer and beauty, but that she was a world-class lover, one who heaped affection on him each time they were together.

The night before Harold's team was to open the season they met at the ranch to spend time together. When it was time to leave Harold had kissed Sarah goodbye and walked away. He had walked ten feet toward his car when a lasso fell over his head and stopped at his waist.

Harold felt the rope tighten and was pulled backwards. He turned, smiled at Sarah, and let her pull him to her. She dropped the lasso, put her arms around him, and kissed him passionately. She said, "I have you now Harold Gatewood, and you are not going to get away."

He laughed and said, "I don't want to get away."

They kissed again and they made plans to see each other when Sarah returned from her next competition in Nashville, Tennessee.

Chapter 18

Season Opener

May 1

HAROLD HAD MET HIS TEAMMATES, renewed his friendship with his old teammate and now manager Scott Binder, and had rounded into baseball playing shape over the last few weeks. He was now ready for the season opener.

Unlike his strikeouts in his first at bats in Japan and Beijing, Harold fared much better in Hayward, Arizona. In his first plate appearance for the Hummingbirds Harold had hit a long homerun, four-hundred-twenty feet from home plate, to right-center field, on the first pitch he had seen. He knew he was back.

After the game he met Sarah who had returned from another rodeo in Portland, Oregon. They spent a glorious evening together, topped off with special lovemaking.

Harold was feeling good and was happy to be back in baseball. Other people in the world were not feeling good, and were very unhappy. President Nazoa of Venezuela was still knee-deep in problems. Ekain Koldo and the AIO were still battling for Basque independence. Mateo Amon was still heartbroken over his daughter Sofia's death.

Fabbri Durante was still fuming at the death of his assassin Baldovino "The Barber" Gioele. Rafael Carmelo of the Carmelo cartel was still upset about the slowdown in his cocaine shipments to America and Canada. Lino Pascual was still planning to take over the Mountain Producers cartel from Mateo Amon. And, Russian contract killer Stanislav Yuli was still waiting on the word from Mateo Amon to kill Lino Pascual.

President Leal Servidor of Mexico was faring better as he had established good working relations with the new president of the United States and was starting to gain leverage against the Salvador Masas drug cartel, which was upsetting the "Stinging Hornet" immensely.

The American people were doing much better as they had elected a new president who was not a member of the Washington elite. He was already making progress in reversing the disasters of the eight years of his predecessor's reign of terror.

America felt hopeful that they could stop the flow of drugs and illegal immigrants into the country, and reclaim the principles that had made the country the most special place on earth. Each dawn the day looked brighter than it had for the eight years of the thankfully-now-out-of-office ex-president.

Little did the citizenry know that the ex-president, who was named the worst president in American history, had set up shop close to the oval office to plan his return to power. He was plotting a silent takeover, a quiet coup, of the reins of power in the next election. He planned to do it without firing a shot, but by stuffing the ballot box and gaining control through a Manchurian-style candidate who would follow his orders and further his radical agenda designed to wipe out the country's history and the constitutional principles that were its cornerstones.

His name was Lance Edwards. He had been a radical in college, sending more time organizing protests then showing up in class. He had been given a free pass by his liberal professors. In exchange for his efforts in rabble-rousing he gained high grades and academic honors. He was a dangerous pawn of the most evil groups of anti-American sentiment in the country.

He would have made Karl Marx and Fidel Castro proud. He believed that government control by a few pampered elites, including himself, should be the norm, as they knew better than the unwashed middle class. His efforts had set the country back in every area during his eight years in office.

It would take generations for the country to fully recover from his actions, if it could survive that long. His loyal minions roamed the streets, creating havoc and disrupting decent people's lives. They waited for their next marching order from him. Once received, they were off to another protest march.

His army of out-of-control lawyers and law-writing judicial activists issued business and citizen-rights- crippling regulations by the thousands in an attempt to circumvent the legal system and gain power through the courts and government to get what they could not earn at the ballot box.

They were a dangerous bunch, and Edwards was the figurehead for the powerful people behind the movement who wanted a one-world government. Even the CIO did not know what they were dealing with as they were continually distracted by the movement's designed disruption of the social order.

Edwards believed in overloading the social systems to cause a collapse in the economic structure of the country. As with all of his actions and schemes, he enjoyed the immunity and lack of scrutiny and criticism by the mainstream press, which gave him freedom to lie over and over until it became part of the lexicon of the country, and was taken as fact.

His fifth column support of loyal, like-minded disrupters desired to undermine and destroy the country, and then make it over in the form they desired.

Edwards was dangerous, and his actions needed to be watched, before it was too late to stop him, and the movement he represented.

Gatewood was happy he was out of the espionage business. He had done his duty as a good citizen and he was now concentrating on his comeback, and enjoying his time with Sarah Belleza. He would let the CIO deal with Lance Edwards and his motley crew of power and control-hungry associates.

Chapter 19

The Fountain of Youth

June 1

THE HUMMINGBIRDS WERE RED HOT. They had been playing great baseball. They were leading their division by five games and were already starting to pull away from the other teams in the West division of the ANNM. They were getting great pitching, good defense, and were riding the hot-hitting bat of Harold Gatewood to victory after victory.

Harold was hitting .388, and had amassed nineteen homeruns and thirty-six runs-batted-in in the first twenty games. Scouts from the major league teams were making their initial pass through the league and were asking themselves if Gatewood had visited the mythical Ponce de Leon Fountain of Youth since his forced retirement from baseball.

Harold was having fun again, and he and Sarah were becoming very close. She had told him that she loved him. But he had not yet reached that level of conversation and feeling. They were a nice match. She was fun to be with, and had a nice sense of humor.

She was also smart enough to let Harold have his private time, and would remain still when he wanted peace and quiet to think and relax. She was also very ticklish, which was much to Harold's liking, as he could find an easy spot to tickle her and make her laugh.

She was usually out every other week on the rodeo circuit, flying to major competitions and then returning to Hayward to relax and be with Harold. His road trips were two weeks long. He would ride the team bus for two weeks and come back ready for a rest at home. The couple rarely went out as they both were road weary when they came home.

Harold's trips to the ballpark in Hayward were different from his days in Tokyo, Beijing, and Seoul, as he now had to drive the four miles across town to Hummingbird Stadium rather than walk.

Before heading to the ballpark Harold checked his voicemail and heard a message from Rick Owens. "Harold, I hear you are back in baseball and are going great guns. Congratulations. I know you are near Tucson, Arizona.

Please call me when you get a chance. I want to ask you something. Harold, we need help."

Gatewood shook his head and thought, "Not now. I am doing too well in my comeback attempt to do anything for the CIO." He then headed to the ballpark. He would call Owens tomorrow.

In Washington, D.C. the CIO was in a tizzy. Their flow of information from the Dominican Republic had fallen off and more drugs were now entering America and Canada. Also, the border near Arizona had recently sprung a leak, and a massive supply of cocaine had made its way to the streets of Phoenix. The CIO needed a plumber to plug the leak. Gatewood's name had come up in conversation between Rick Owens and Terry Robbins.

"Sir, the amount of the last drug shipment through the Southern Arizona border near Tucson is now estimated to be over fifty tons of cocaine.'

'What was it last month Terry?"

"It was very small, a little over five tons."

"It has increased ten times."

"Yes. Something is going on."

"Have we had any surveillance reports?'

"No. No one knows how it is happening."

"Do we have any agents in the area?"

"No. They are all working in the Phoenix area."

"I understand. Usually, there are more problems to solve in large metropolitan areas."

"Rick, we think that the Salvador Masas cartel is behind the increased shipments. They may have changed their routes."

"The Stinging Hornet. He is a tough one to stop."

"Yes. He has the best equipment on the market, and the most loyal, cutthroat employees in Mexico."

"Let's try to see if we can put an additional set of eyes on the border area near the national park."

"Okay."

"Do you have anyone in mind who can do that for us Terry?"

"No."

"I read where Gatewood is now back in baseball and playing for some minor league team near Tucson."

"Do you think he would help us?"

"Maybe. But I feel guilty asking him. After what he has been through I am always afraid he will be killed."

"Should we contact him Sir?"

"Let me do it. I will see if he will help us."

In Hayward, Arizona Gatewood had put Rick Owens call out of his thoughts, driven to the ballpark, dressed, and proceeded to lead he Hummingbirds to a three to two win over the Stratton Ravens of the eastern division of the ANNM. This had been the last game of the home stand and the Hummingbirds would be leaving on a two week road trip tomorrow morning.

After the game he found Sarah sitting on his living room couch. When he entered she stood up, walked to him, put her arms around his waist and kissed him. She said that she had heard the game on the radio and congratulated him on driving in the winning run.

She said, "That deserves a reward." She then took his hand and led him to the bedroom for a night of wonderful lovemaking. She stayed the night, dropped Harold off at the ballpark so he did not have to leave his car there for two weeks, then went home to pack for a rodeo competition in Seattle, Washington.

Before leaving him she said, "Honey, I will pick you up when you get back. We can spend the night together." She then kissed him and drove away.

Harold boarded the team bus and took his usual seat on the right side of the bus, in the half-way area from the front. He sat down by the window and thought about Rick Owens' phone call. He said, "It can wait. I will call him when we get to Denton, Mexico to play the Desperadoes."

The bus driver sat patiently behind the wheel for ten minutes until the last person to board walked up the steps and into the bus. It was the eccentric, somewhat demented old character who thought he was Billy The Kid. He was an institution for the Hummingbirds as he bid farewell to the team before they left on every road trip.

At home games he sat behind home plate and led the crowd in cheers for the Hummingbirds when they made a great play in the field or hit a home run. He was a self-appointed cheerleader for the team, and drew many fans to the park, as they wanted to watch his antics.

The bus rolled out of Hayward and the team was off to Mexico and New Mexico for two weeks of road games. Gatewood closed his eyes and dreamed of making his successful comeback to the big leagues. This road trip would be an additional brick in the wall of his journey back.

Chapter 20

"It will work"

May 3

THE DRIVER PULLED THE DARK BLACK LIMOUSINE into the dusty backroad, and followed it uphill for a mile, where he pulled into a lane and parked in front of a metal building that served as the training headquarters for the AIO near La Merdedur De Serpant, Spain.

Ekain Koldo, national Commander of the AIO, got out of the backseat, stretched after a long ride, and asked to see the training officer. He was welcomed with enthusiasm as the camp was buzzing about the mission that Theobaldo Gil had been assigned. Everyone had been waiting for Koldo's return trip, and now he was here.

Koldo asked, "Is agent Gil here?"

"Yes Sir. He is refining his murder-related skills in the garage behind the training office."

"Please take me to him."

"Yes Sir. Please follow me."

The two men found Gil hard at work under a car, which had its hood raised.

Koldo asked, "Are you sleeping under there Gil?"

The agent quickly slid out from under the car and said, "No sir. I am working."

"What are you working on?"

"Sir, I am refining m skills in the fine art of car bombing."

"Very good. Please come with me Gil."

The agent cleaned the oil from his hands and followed Koldo to a vacant area near the training office and sat down when he was ordered to do so.

"Theobaldo, I have come to tell you that it is time for you to do your duty. You will leave tomorrow for America."

"Am I still to take care of Harold Gatewood?"

"Oh yes. Please do as we discussed."

"I am ready Sir."

"Do you remember our conversation?"

"Yes Sir. Kill Gatewood or I will be killed if I fail."

"Good. You understand the importance of the mission them."

"Yes I do."

"He is in Southern Arizona, near Tucson, in a small town named Hayward."

"Okay."

"You are to proceed to Hayward and tail Gatewood. Find out his movements and hangouts."

"Yes Sir."

"As we discussed, he is a creature of habit. You have his file."

"Yes. I have memorized it."

"Eliminate him."

"Sir, I have requested certain items I will need for the completion of my assignment."

"Those will be supplied by our good friend Salvador Masas."

"How will I receive them?"

"One of his couriers will bring them to you. You will meet him in a place to be named later. You will keep the items in your possession until you need them."

"I understand."

"Are you sure that you have considered every possibility that could lead to failure?"

"Yes, I have Sir."

"I want to be assured that your plan is sound. Please cover it in detail with me."

Gil then went over his operation plan, and also covered the potential roadblocks to success and ow he would handle any setbacks.

Koldo agreed the plan was sound and then asked if there were any questions.

"Yes Sir. What are the details of my escape plan?"

"After completing the mission you will be escorted to Mexico by the same Masas cartel operate that brought you the materials you requested."

"What then?"

"You will be flown to Mexico on one of Masas's private lanes, or you will be placed on commercial airlines from Mexico City to Madrid. If there are no hints of you being involved in Gatewood's murder you will fly commercially. Proper documents will be furnished by the Masas cartel."

"I understand."

"Agent Gil, I want to be reassured once more that your plan will work."

"Sir, it will work. I will bet my life on it."

"You are betting your life on it agent Gil."

When all details of the mission had been agreed upon Koldo said goodbye and headed back to Madrid.

Theobaldo Gil returned to the garage and continued to brush up on his training. Koldo's final words stayed in the front of his mind. He was betting his life that the plan would work.

Chapter 21

"A fine day for a walk"

May 4

STANISLAV YULI WAS AN ASSASSIN IN THE RUSSIAN MOB. His employer was one of the five biggest crime families in the world. His "family" was the Russian mob called Solntsevskeya Bratva, which was a decentralized group of ten organizations that dealt drugs, especially heroin, and was involved in human trafficking.

He had progressed through the chairs of the organization to become a hitman. He had killed in the line of duty in his mother country of Russia, several countries in Eastern Europe, Spain, Portugal, France, and Belgium. He became expendable to the Mafia because he knew information that could present a problem if he ever talked to the authorities.

After he entered the world of self-employment and proceeded to perform contract killings in America, Canada, Haiti, Sweden, Finland, and Australia. He was a renaissance man when it came to killing.

He was relaxing in the beach near his home in Soleil Ville, France when his cell phone rang.

"Hello, this is Mateo Amon."
"Yes Sir."
"Did you receive my payment?"
"Yes Mr. Amon."
"It is time."
"When do you want me to leave?"
"Tomorrow."
"Very well."
"Do you remember the instructions?"
"Yes Sir."
"Do you see any new complications?"
"No Sir."
"Do not fail."
"I will not fail."
"Will you call me when it is done?"

"No, you will hear it from your sources, or on the news."

"Do you have any questions?"

"No. But, I want to remind you about the timeframe for submitting final payment."

Mateo Amon replied, "I understand the timeframe and will meet it."

"Very good. I will perform this task and look forward to handling the second matter you mentioned."

"Yes. Once the first mission is done we will proceed to the Gatewood matter."

"Excellent. Good day Sir."

"Good day."

The next morning Yuli was on a flight to Caracas, Venezuela. He relaxed in his seat and ordered a Grigori Russian vodka, then a second, and then a third. He loved his vodka, and like many Russians, he was addicted to alcohol. He was a vicious drunk, and often took out his repressed hatred of his mother and his younger brother on whoever was in his vicinity. In Caracas, he staggered off the plane, picked up his rental car, drove to the hotel, and crashed into bed for an early night's sleep.

The next morning he headed to the mountains to scout the area where his target was located. He passed the small medical clinic where Diego Ramirez had killed the doctor who had treated Luisa Gaicia, and continued up the mountain road toward his target's location. He scouted his target's movements for two days and then formalized his plan.

The next morning Lino Pascual arose, had breakfast, spoke to his management people about the outlined activities of the day, and then waked out into the sunshine. He let the heat of the sun hit him in the face, and took in its rejuvenating energy.

He closed his eyes and thought of his work, the cartel's recent setbacks, and how he could change the operation once he was in charge of the cartel. He opened his eyes and said, "A fine day for a walk."

Lino then told his assistant that he was going to take his morning walk around the cartel complex to check on the morning's work progress. He stopped at each department and made a visual and verbal assessment of the completed and pending work. He determined that the work was progressing ahead of schedule.

He turned and headed toward the main office, ready to dive into the projects that lay on his desk. He walked three steps, and no more.

Stanislav Yuli sighted his sniper rifle scope in on the area between Pascual's eyes and gently squeezed the trigger. The bullet was near the target before a sound rang out. Upon arrival the bullet, the cartridge casing had been ejected from the rifle and had fallen to the ground. By the time the bullet had torn through the front lobe of his brain Pascual was on his way out of his earthly presence.

Yuli had chambered another round in case his first shot had not been true, but it was not needed as Pascual was in the process of falling to the ground, dead.

The assassin watched Pascual's body to make sure he was dead. Two cartel members ran from the main office to their leader's prone, dead body to see if they could be of help. It was no use. He was gone.

Yuli's mission was done. He rushed down his escape path to his vehicle and drove away, the tires kicking up dust as he sped down the hill. He reached the bottom of the hill and drove the four miles to the paved highway that led back to Caracas, Venezuela.

Once in Caracas, he immediately caught the next plane back to France. At the airport he walked to his car, and drove the thirty miles to his home. The next morning he checked to make sure the last half of his fee had been deposited in his offshore account, and then drove to his beloved beach near the ocean.

In Elle Se Cayo, Venezuela, Mateo Amon had arisen, heard the news that Lino Pascual had been killed, and had made the last half of his contract payment to Stanislav Yuli. He walked to the front porch and let the bright sunshine hit his face. He thought of his departed daughter Sofia and smiled as he remembered her beauty and pleasantness.

He called for his wife to join him on the porch. She did so, and he said, "It is done. We now have one target left, Harold Gatewood."

She put her hand on is shoulder and smiled. Mateo knew her thoughts and feelings without her having to explain them. He hugged her tightly and looked up at the sun. He then said, "It is a fine day for a walk." He took his wife's hand and they strolled down the steps and toward the road in front of the house. The walked away, hand in hand.

Chapter 22

No Net Gain

May 4

AIO AGENT THEOBALDO GIL HAD DRIVEN to Madrid after National Commander Ekain Koldo had visited the training camp in La Merdedur De Serpant to make sure the details of the mission were clear in his agent's mind.

After checking into his hotel, Theobaldo reviewed the details of his mission and thought about the warning he had been given if success was not the outcome of his trip to Arizona, in the United States. If he did not kill Gatewood he was as sure as dead himself. He had come to understand a new definition of the word pressure. He brushed the thought as he was confident that Gatewood would be eliminated.

He arrived in Phoenix, Arizona, on the same day that Stanislav Yuli had left Caracas, Venezuela. There had been no net gain in the number of assassins working on May fourth. Gil picked up his rental car, and headed South to Tucson. Upon arrival he checked into his motel room and then drove to nearby Hayward.

He drove to Gatewood's apartment building, and surveyed its layout. Gatewood was living in a first floor apartment, number 1E. His bedroom was not visible from the outside back window of the building.

Gil had been advised that Gatewood followed a set schedule and was a creature of habit. Due to the distance between his apartment and the Hummingbird's ballpark Gatewood was now driving to work. He had driven his own car to Arizona and would notice anything unusual in its appearance. He was spending most all of his free time with a beautiful girl named Sarah Belleza, whose parents had grown up in the area and were of Native American and Spanish descent.

Gil realized that if Gatewood and Belleza were together it would be difficult to successfully launch an in-person attack, as she would be able to identify him as the killer. He would have to kill both of them if he attacked in person. As much as he would like to kill Gatewood in person Gil now had to rule out that option.

The apartment building was located in an open area, with no cover anywhere that could be used for concealment. He would have to shoot

Gatewood from his parked rental car if he was going to kill him at the apartment building. He would run the risk of being spotted and identified if he tried that approach.

He drove the route that Gatewood probably used to get to and from the ballpark, looking for a concealed spot to shoot him from as he drove by. The road was in the open, on the outskirts of town. Traffic was fairly heavy, which would create the same problems as those that existed at the apartment building, plus complicate his flight from the murder scene.

The ballpark was set in an open area, and surrounded by the parking lot and nothing else for miles. That option was too risky to consider as the killing location as he would be spotted immediately.

He then drove to Sarah Belleza's parents' ranch, where the couple spent time together. Again, it was in an open area, the desert. The same problems existed as at the other locations. No, this location would not work either.

He next considered killing Gatewood while he was on a road trip playing other teams in Mexico and New Mexico. He would be spread out over a vast area if he followed the team around looking for an opportunity to kill Gatewood in any of the eleven other cities in the ANNM the league. Scouting each city for an opportunity would take too long and be exhausting. Plus, his escape route would be compromised, and be much too dangerous.

Gil also thought about placing a rattlesnake in Gatewood's apartment or car, but that option could be averted if the snake was found. Plus, the file on Gatewood mentioned that he had a fear of snakes, especially after his experience with a seones viper that had been put in his hotel room in San Toro De Lidia, Spain. Gatewood was supposedly so shaken with the experience that he checked under his bed each night to make sure no snakes were in the room. No, snakes would not do the trick.

He would have to revert to his specialty, which he had used many times. He was now sure that option was his best one. Gatewood and the Hummingbirds were still on a road trip so he had ten days to perfect his weapon of death and place it in the killing location.

Gil smiled as he thought of the scene when the weapon would do its job. He envisioned Gatewood's immediate horror when the weapon of death was put into action. He would be close by to watch the glorious event, and then he would meet his contact from the Masas cartel and make his way out of Arizona and return to Spain as a conquering hero, the man who had killed Harold Gatewood for the AIO and the Basque people who had been demanding the ballplayer's head on a platter.

His work for the day was done. In the morning he would start on his fail-safe plan.

Chapter 23

The Return

May 14

THE HUMMINGBIRDS WERE SUCCESSFUL on their two week road trip, winning eleven of fourteen games in New Mexico and Mexico. Gatewood continued his hot hitting raising his batting average to .396, slugging five home runs, and driving in, eighteen runs. He was feeling great, and looking forward to returning to Hayward to be with Sarah Belleza.

Sarah was waiting for him when the bus pulled into the ballpark parking lot. He departed the bus, and saw her standing by her car with a broad smile on her face. He walked to her, put his arms around her, and kissed her. She told him she loved him, and for the first time, Gatewood said, "I love you too."

She tingled with excitement as she had finally heard the words she had been longing to hear. She kissed him passionately and then told him that she was going to spend the night with him. As they drove to his apartment, she told him that she had been reducing her times in the barrel-racing event, and had tied the world record at the practice corral at the ranch.

He was happy for her progress and told her that she would soon duplicate the feat in her next rodeo event, at Baton Rouge, Louisiana, next week. He said that she would be setting a new world record in the event soon, and he volunteered to work with her at the ranch to further reduce her times.

Sarah told him that she had been following the Hummingbird games on the trip and knew that he was tearing the cover off the ball. Harold said that he was feeling great and had seen an increasing number of major league scouts in the stands at the games.

She asked what that meant and he said, "I don't really know. They don't talk much about who they are looking at. They may be scouting some of my teammates or the opposition. But, I am also hoping they are also watching me very closely."

Sarah said, "What will happen?"

Gatewood responded, "Hopefully my contract will be purchased from the Hummingbirds and I will make it back to the big leagues."

"Where?"

He laughed and said, "Anywhere. Or, they may send me to double A or triple A to see how I would fare there. Then I might be called up to the majors if I perform well."

"What will happen to us?"

"Honey, nothing is going to happen to us."

"I hope not."

Sarah eased the car to a stop in the apartment parking lot and said, "Harold, I love you, I want to be with you for the rest of our lives."

He kissed her and said, "That is what I want also."

They walked upstairs to his apartment where he threw his gym bag on the floor next to the couch and picked up the mail that Sarah had left on the kitchen room table. She took the mail from his hands threw it on the table and said, "Later." She then led him to the bedroom where they made wonderful, meaningful love.

They slept until morning, repeated their lovemaking, and showered together. She started to fix breakfast and realized that there was no milk. She said, "Harold, I am going to run to the grocery store and a few things."

Gatewood threw her his car keys and said, "Take my car. It has been sitting for two weeks while I have been gone and needs to be driven."

The car keys flew through the air and into Sarah's hands. She smiled and said, "See, I have good hands too. Just like a catcher."

"No, your hands are way to pretty to be a catcher."

"She laughed, kissed him and said she would be back soon.

She headed toward Harold's car, smiling and singing as she went. She opened the door and eased into the driver's side seat. She placed the key in the lock, then relaxed and thought. "I am about to set a new world's record in barrel race, and I am with the man I love. My life is perfect." She then turned the key in the ignition.

Upstairs, Harold was again looking at the pile of mail that had arrived in his absence. He was shocked by the sound of a loud explosion. He walked to the window and looked out at the parking lot. He screamed in horror, "Sarah !"

He stood frozen at the window, looking at what used to be his car. Flames and black smoke were rushing skyward, and pieces of metal from his car were scattered around the parking lot. His eyes scanned the parking lot to find Sarah. He hoped she had not been near the explosion.

He could not find her. He stood motionless trying to locate her. He was in a daze but saw three people who had left their apartment running toward the scene. They were joined by a fourth person walking toward the fire and mangled steel remains of his car, from the side of the parking lot. He finally realized what has happening, dropped his mail, and rushed toward the scene.

The four people had now reached the car ahead of him and were standing, gawking at the burning remains of the car. As Harold approached the burning car he was still hopeful Sarah had somehow not been in the car when it exploded. His hopes were shattered when he saw a burning corpse in the driver's seat.

Sarah Belleza, the beautiful woman of Tohono O'odhan and Spanish blood lines of her parents, was dead.

Harold looked at the faces of the four people at the scene. Three of the people were concerned, and looking confused at what had happened.

The fourth man had a smile on his face. Gatewood locked eyes with the man and realized he knew who he was. He had seen his picture in the AIO file of field agents when he had been recruited and trained by the CIO for his mission in the Dominican Republic.

The fourth person at the scene was AIO assassin Theobaldo Gil.

Gil had been waiting for the bomb to detonate. He had been sitting in his car around the corner of the apartment building. He had chosen a spot where he could hear the explosion but be out of sight when it went off, as he did not want to be seen near the building.

While Gil had waited, he had thought about how he had rigged the car bomb while Gatewood was on the two week road trip with the Hummingbirds. He had chosen to wire the bomb to the ignition system of the vehicle as it would go off when the key was turned in the lock.

He preferred that system, even though it could be defused if it were found before detonation. He had correctly assumed that Gatewood would not suspect that he was being trailed and chosen for assassination. He also had assumed that Gatewood would be trying to catch up on all of the events that had taken place in his two-week absence and would not be thinking about being killed.

Gil had realized that he would now be the hero of the AIO, the man had finally killed Harold Gatewood. Despite knowing better, and not leaving the scene, he could not resist the pleasure of seeing Gatewood's dead, burning corpse in the burning car. He had walked to the car to view his fine work.

The two men were now standing less than ten feet away, looking at each other with surprise. Looks of hate immediately followed. Gill knew it was now or never if he was going to kill his target. He drew his pistol from its holster and started to fire at Gatewood.

Gatewood, who had learned the hard way, always carried a sidearm, and did likewise, and prepared to fire at Gill. Four shots rang out in rapid succession. Gatewood had drawn and fired the first shot in a style that would have made Wyatt Earp and his co-harts at the gunfight at the O. K. Corral proud.

His first shot had hit Gil one inch above his heart. The second shot, which had hit the ground in front of him because Gil he had drawn and fired too late, had belonged to Gil.

The third and fourth shots had been pumped into Gil's chest as he fell to the ground. Gatewood's aim had been true on all three of his shots.

Gil was dead.

Harold waited for the police and firemen, sitting on the grass until they arrived. He had holstered his pistol and was sitting quietly, in disbelief that Sarah was gone. After being questioned by the police, he called Sarah's parents to tell them the tragic news, and then walked back to his apartment where he silently sat until it was time to go to the ballpark for the night's game.

Chapter 24

"I will"

May 15

GATEWOOD FOUND COMFORT AT THE HUMMINGBIRD BALLPARK. His manager Scott Binder and his teammates offered their condolences and asked if he was alright. He had said yes, even though he was not. He went through the motions during the game. He read in the paper the next day that he had gone one for four, but he did not remember anything about the game.

He was up early thinking about Sarah. He waited until eleven thirty a.m. then made a call to Rick Owens at the CIO.

"Hello Rick. This is Harold Gatewood."

"Are you alright Harold? I just read in the paper about Sarah being killed. I am sorry."

"Thank you. It was Theobaldo Gil from the AIO."

"Yes. I heard that from the Hayward and Tucson police."

"Rick, I want to help you get the AIO and the Masas cartel."

"Are you sure?"

"Yes. What can I do for the CIO?"

"The Salvador Masas cartel is running drugs and illegal immigrants across the border near Tucson and flooding the streets of Phoenix with cocaine and heroin. We need someone to monitor the area South of Tucson, here you are now. Will you help us?"

"I will."

"You will work with the border guards and with Jack Taylor, who is on a plane headed to the area today. Mainly, you will be watching the area for airplane drop-offs of drugs in remote areas, truck movement in and out of the area to and from Phoenix, and the movement of illegal aliens by the cartel's coyotes."

"I can do that in my time before and maybe after the ballgames."

"Mainly, you will reporting what you see to Jack Taylor. He will take things from there."

"Great. Have him call me when he gets in."

"Harold, thanks, and remember, be careful."
"I will."
'I hope so."
"What else is going on that might impact the situation here?"
"We have still been following Aamir Jawdat."
"What is he doing?"
"Harold, I still see him at the running track still sporting his new jogging suit and tennis shoes that he wore when I first saw him. Obviously, he is still not jogging, as the clothes and shoes show no wear, only coming out of the closet to be worn when he goes to the track to receive or leave a message under the rock. His actions have drawn more attention in the CIO office building, as he is now under official surveillance.

Our actions have yielded positive results, as Aamir was frequently seen at the park, and in a coffee shop near his home in Arlington, Virginia where he buys a newspaper from his waitress and then leaves newspaper in his booth when he left. His waitress, a woman of Middle Eastern descent, picks up the newspaper and places it in her purse in the employee restroom. Surveillance on the woman has yielded a connection to a second man, also of Middle Eastern descent, who receives the newspaper from the coffee shop.

It was obvious that notes, and information, are being passed from Jawdat, through the waitress, to the man who is obviously his contact. I have also learned that Aamir is meeting other Middle Eastern men at a prayer meeting each Sunday. A warrant had been issued to allow surveillance on the group at the prayer meeting. Many possible subjects have been identified are having ties to a terrorist organization with ties to Lebanon.

More disturbing facts have been uncovered when Jawdat, who has presented himself as a meek man afraid of firearms, is regularly participating in firearms practice at a farm outside Arlington with his friends from the prayer meetings. The farm is owned by a wealthy businessman also of Middle Eastern descent who lives in the Arlington area. I have ordered that all of the subjects should be monitored in an effort to gain more information, as I felt Jawdat was connected to a terror cell that had a future mission in mind.

I have Terry Robbins heading the internal investigation of Jawdat. He says that there is no doubt that the group is probable terrorist cell that is planning something big. We just don't know what it is yet. We are monitoring the members' phone conversations and there is a lot of chatter.

Obviously, Aamir Jawdat is a deep-cover mole here at the CIO. He has enjoyed access to needed information on CIO operations and activities, and has been able to give that information to the USFF, the Syrian freedom fighters, and has been able to parlay his actions into a money-making endeavor for himself. He was recently caught on tape talking to his wife about how his latest payoff as allowed them to pay off their mortgage. She is helping his efforts, and also committing treason.

He is a paid agent for a terrorist group whose interests are in opposition to the United States. He is committing treason under the Espionage Act number 18 U.S.C. section 794 c, which carries a life in prison sentence. He is a dangerous man who is harming America, and he is now as free as a bird. Soon, that will change, and both he and his wife will be shamed and prosecuted.

Jawdat does not know we have been monitoring his actions. He also does not know that Jack Taylor, who had saved your life several times Harold, is also tailing him. Taylor laughs at Jawdat, because he thinks he is outsmarting us. Jack says that the time will soon come Jawdat will not be smiling or laughing when the CIO and the American justice system doles out he and his wife's punishment for their treason. Taylor vows that we will be right there to close the trap on Jawdat when the time is right.

We believe that he is also working with the Masas cartel in Mexico on setting up more terrorist training camps near the American border."

Gatewood replied, "The Stinging Hornet. I have hated that guy since I first saw him on Mexican President Alto Roble's yacht in Cabo San Lucas."

"You are well aware of how dangerous he is."

"Yes, I know all about him. I consider him human debris that needs to be thrown on top of the trash pile. He is responsible for so many deaths. Bodies are piling up everywhere from the effects of his drug distribution system."

"You hate him because of his illegal activities?"

"Yes. Plus, I have a personal reason to want him dead. He hooked Jeong Eun on cocaine. She died in Mexico City. She was a friend of Yeong Hyeon and I."

Gatewood paused and thought of the first time she had seen her on Alto Roble's yacht in Cabo San Lucas. He then thought about the first encounter.

He had requested, and received, room one hundred from his outfitter. He laughed when he looked at the room number on the door and thought, "I hope there is not a terrible surprise in my room. I am not sure but I don't think seones vipers live in Cabo San Lucas so I should be safe."

When he opened the door, he was not greeted by an unsafe sight, but a wonderful one. Standing in the middle of the room, wearing one of his long-sleeve white shirts that was unbuttoned in the front, and nothing else, was the gorgeous North Korean deckhand Jeong Eun. She smiled and said, "Hello Harold, I have been waiting for you for a very, very long time. Please come here."

Harold threw his room key on the small table by the door, and obliged, covering the distance between them in record time. He smiled at her, took her right hand into his left, looked at her beautiful body and said, "How long have you been waiting for me?"

She put her left hand around his neck, drew him close to her, and said, "Since the first time I saw you when you arrived in Pyongyang, North Korea. She then kissed him, led him to the bed, helped him out of his shirt, then his slacks, then the rest of his clothing, and turned back the covers and helped him, then herself, under the covers. Harold started to talk, but she put her right index finger up to his lips to silence his comments, and said, "Later."

The couple was locked in romantic pleasure for two hours before they decided they should be properly introduced. "Harold, I meant what I said. I have wanted to be with you since I saw you at the supreme leader's palace."

"I didn't see you."

"I was forbidden to be near you, as Yeong Hyeon was assigned to be your contact, and your seductress. I wanted the mission."

"I don't even know what to say. Where was your job, and where were you in the palace all the time I was there?"

"I was in charge of helping Yeong prepare for the mission with you. My room was across the courtyard from her room, but I could see your room. I would watch you, and curse my bad luck for not being chosen to be with you. I did all of the research on your career, habits, likes, dislikes, fears, and hopes. I knew all about you months before you were asked to train our national baseball team."

"Gatewood laughed and said, "And you still wanted to be with me?"

"Yes. I love everything about you."

"That is very high praise from such a beautiful, interesting woman."

"Thank you Harold."

"How did you end up here in Cabo San Lucas?"

"After you left our national baseball team played their season. As you could tell immediately, they were terrible. They had a dismal season and embarrassed the supreme leader."

Gatewood laughed, stroked her beautiful, short, shiny black hair, and said, "They were awful weren't they?"

Jeong joined in the laughter and soon both were laughing so hard that they could not talk. Gatewood finally regained his breath and asked her, "How did you end up in Mexico, and on the yacht?"

"The Supreme Leader Jun Hanuel blamed me for the failure of the national team, exiled me, and sent me as a present to Mexican President Alto Roble."

"That is terrible. It was not your fault."

"He always needs a scapegoat. Luckily, he did not decide to kill me."

"Are you alright now?"

"Being a slave to Roble is a terrible life. But, I am happy now that you are here, and we are together at this moment."

"Why did you come to my room?"

"Because I volunteered for the mission, and because I have loved you from the time I started preparing the file on you in North Korea."

"That is very flattering. Are you disappointed?"

She kissed him passionately, pulled him down on the bed again and said, "No, not at all." She continued to kiss him and repeated her comments, "No, not at all Harold." They made love again for an hour, finally taking a break from their glorious, passionate love-making.

Gatewood was jolted back to the present when he heard Rick Owens say, "Harold, don't let your personal hatred for Salvador Masas get in the way of our mission."

"I won't Rick"

They finished the details related to Harold's role in the mission and Owens wished him well. After hanging up the phone Harold said, "Mission or not, if I get a chance to kill Masas I will."

Chapter 25
Failure

May 16

TWELVE MEN, PATRIOTS AT HEART, trudged up the stairs to the office of the AIO terrorist organization. As their national committee grew with each new man's arrival, they all said their helloes, and took their appropriate seats at a large rectangular-shaped table.

On the wall above the chair at the far end of the table was the red, green and white flag of the Basque people. The tall, black-haired mustachioed man rose from his chair and spoke.

"Welcome fellow freedom fighters. Long Live the Basque people."

"Thank you Sir. We salute you."

To all of the committee members he looked much older, with some gray hair now on his sideburns and the top of his head. His face was drawn and wrinkles had appeared where they were not allowed in the past. Even when he spoke his voice was not as strong as in the past, a mere shell of itself now. His spirit had been broken over the last few years, the timeframe in which their hated enemy, Harold Gatewood, had entered their sphere of operation.

He was a broken, failed man who now faced the ouster from his current position unless he could salvage the Gatewood situation. He was on his way out, and he and everyone else knew it.

The topic of the meeting was the failure of Operacion Para Romper, the name of which had appropriately been chosen because the translation meant Operation Go For Broke. The translation mirrored Ekain Koldo's situation perfectly. The operation had failed miserably. Theobaldo Gil's carelessness had led to his death after being shot by Harold Gatewood.

Koldo covered the details of the disaster with the committee and then became quiet. It was a pitiful sight for the committee members to witness. Finally, the Deputy National commander spoke and expressed his disappointment with the outcome of the mission. He then opened the floor to the regional commanders for discussion.

The tone of the discussion was angry. It quickly became very personal, and Koldo was crucified unmercifully. He held up as best as he could, but he was being humiliated in front of his peers, who had turned on him for the many failures of the AIO agents' attempts to kill Gatewood.

Koldo tried to mount a defense but he was beaten down with each attempt. He was a failure, and he was ready to throw in the towel. His basic nature was not to give up, but he was ready to put his personal torture and his failure to slay his own "white whale" Harold Gatewood to rest.

The discussion was still white-hot as committee members were screaming, pounding the desk with their fists, and demanding Koldo's head. Ekain Koldo loved the AIO and the Basque people and he was willing to step down. The ugly scene was still in process when he stood, laid a piece of paper on the desk that contained his resignation, and quietly walked to the door and down the stairs into the Madrid night air. He breathed in the oxygen and thought. He then said, "Yes, it was the thing to do."

Chapter 26

The Call

June 29

JACK TAYLOR HAD ARRIVED IN HAYWARD and started his work with Gatewood monitoring the drug deliveries and the illegal immigration movements across the border in the area. Harold Gatewood had tailed off a bit from his hot start but was still hitting .374 and drawing a crowd of scouts at the Hummingbird games.

Fabbri Durante's choice of soldati to eliminate Gatewood, Gavino Romilda, had been killed while on a mission in Rome. Fabbri had no other soldier qualified at the moment to take his place so Gatewood appeared to be safe from the crime family's vengeance. Ekain Koldo was out as National Commander of the AIO.

Gatewood drove to the ballpark and started to change into his uniform when Scott Binder walked by and asked him to come to his office. Binder started the conversation.

"Harold we have been friends and teammates for a long time. I have seen you at your best and at your worst. I hope you will take what I have to tell you in its proper context."

Harold's heart sank. He had herd similar words when his manager for the Tokyo Cardinals, Katashi Katsu, whose name meant firm victory in Japanese, had called him into his office. He had met Katsu in Cuba at the World Baseball Games, when he was managing the Japanese National Team, and Harold was scouting the games for the Major League Baseball.

Katsu respected Harold's appreciation for the game, his abilities, his lifestyle, his competiveness, his desire to win, and the fact that he was a student of the game. He planned to use Harold as a designated hitter and platoon player against left-handed pitching, as a left fielder, third baseman, and first baseman, and as a defensive replacement as a catcher, if his arm was sound.

The mutual admiration society was in play, as Harold respected Katashi's style of managing, his baseball knowledge, his love for the game, and his character as a family man. Harold knew he could play for him, and that they would form a winning team.

Harold had done spectacularly for Katsu and the Tokyo Cardinals and they had released him, with many of the same words Scott Binder had just said. He held his breath again and waited for Binder to speak.

"You don't have to finish dressing Harold."

"Gatewood's heart sank again.

"Your contract has been purchased by Phoenix in the major leagues."

Gatewood relaxed, smiled and asked, "Are they sending me to double A or triple A?"

"Neither."

"I am being sent all the way down below A ball?"

"No. You are going to play for Pat Sullivan in the big leagues. You got the call to return to the big leagues."

Harold jumped from his chair and yelled in glee. He and Scott Binder then hugged each other and Harold told him how much he appreciated Scott's confidence in him in giving him his chance to get to back in the major leagues.

"You earned it Harold. Pat Sullivan wants you to be in Phoenix tomorrow for the evening game."

Harold was on cloud nine as he walked to his locker, dressed , wished his teammates well, and headed back to his apartment. He made all of the arrangements for paying his bills, packing, and making sure he left Hayward with the slate clean. He went to bed, but he could not sleep, as he was thinking about his return to where he belonged.

In the morning, he packed the car and headed North to Phoenix. The short drive went quickly. He went to the ballpark and took care of all the details related to his contract, and an apartment. He then ate lunch, checked into a motel, in his requested room of one hundred, for one night, as he would be in his apartment the next day. He relaxed for a while, and then headed back to the ballpark.

Pat Sullivan arrived at the stadium and welcomed Harold to the club. Harold told him how much he appreciated Pat's faith in him and promised to give his all for the team.

Sullivan replied, "I needed help right away Harold. I know you will do everything you can do to help us. By the way, I arranged for you to have uniform number ten, because that was your dad's number when he played on the All-American team that went to England and when he played in the minors."

"Thank you Pat. I appreciate that."

"I have you in the lineup, batting fifth. Have fun and enjoy yourself."

"I will Pat. We'll make things happen."

Harold then went to the locker room, met his teammates, and dressed for the game. He walked up the runway to the dugout, looked at the lineup card on the wall and saw his name in the fifth slot of the batting order as Pat Sullivan had said. He then limbered up, and took batting practice.

Harold then relaxed and took in all of the sights and smells he loved at the ballpark. The grass smelled clean, and the air smelled fresh, better than in the minor leagues. The stadium was beautiful. He looked at the bright blue-colored seats, the green-colored hitting background in centerfield, and the beautiful scoreboard. He was relishing every minute of his comeback.

The game began and Harold watched his teammates go down in order, three outs on weak ground balls to the infielders.

He then went to the area below the stands and stretched, hit ten balls off a hitting tee in the cage, and returned to the dugout.

When the bottom of the second arrived he donned his batting helmet, went to the on-deck circle, and took five practice swings at imaginary swings, reminding himself to keep his head down when he swung. The hitter before him led off the inning with a weak fly ball out to left field.

Harold walked from the on-deck circle and heard his named called, "The next batter is Harold Gatewood, number ten." The crowd of thirty-nine thousand one hundred fans gave him a nice round of applause, all mindful of his second successful comeback to the major leagues and the many tragic, dangerous, and inspirational actions that had marked the last few years of his life.

Harold tipped his hat and then riveted all of his thoughts on the pitcher, a left-hander with a hopping fastball. He stepped into the batter's box and intensely watched the pitcher's throwing arm. The pitcher would up and threw a four-seam fast ball. As it sped toward home plate, Harold watched the seams of the ball, kept his head down, took his stride into the pitch, and sent a screaming line-drive into right-center field for a single.

He rounded first base, smiled, and clenched his fist in glee. After he returned to first base, the first baseman patted him on the thigh with his glove and said, "Welcome back." The first base umpire called timeout and the ball was thrown to the Phoenix dugout as a remembrance of Harold's first hit in his return to the big leagues. The crowd had been watching to see if Harold was ready for his return, as many doubted he could play again due to his age.

With the hit, the crowd erupted and clapped for an extended time. Soon, they were on their feet in a standing ovation. Harold, with his fists clenched, raised both arms above his head and pounded the air in appreciation. Tears rolled down his cheeks as he thought of his dad. He was overcome with emotion.

As he stood looking at the cheering crowd, he suddenly felt a pain in his back, and fell to the ground. He laid in pain on the ground as blood rushed from his chest and back, soaking his uniform and the dirt near him. He labored to breath, and started to sink away. His life flashed before his eyes. He saw his dad, and his deceased wife Akemi, his one true love, and then his eyes closed. He was rushed to the hospital.

On a rooftop a far distance from the stadium a man in a ghillie suit stood up, broke down his sniper's rifle, removed his suit, and placed all of the items in a black-colored plastic bag. He removed his camo-colored face mask and also placed it in the bag.

The man, Ekain Koldo, smiled and said, "I have done what many others could not do. I have killed Harold Gatewood. I will surely be renamed the national commander of the AIO when I return to Madrid."

He then hurried down the stairs to the street and walked to the subway where he boarded his train and headed to his motel far away from the middle of the city. He entered his room and patted himself on the back for his accomplishment. He showered and decided that he should reward himself for his successful mission. He called an escort service and asked that a nice, beautiful young woman be dispatched to his room in an hour.

He listened to the news on television, as the shooting incident was being discussed non-stop. Precisely an hour later a knock was heard at his door. He looked through the door's peephole and smiled. He opened the door and smiled again. His order had arrived. She was a gorgeous black-haired young woman. She walked into the room, holding her hands behind her back.

Koldo said, "Welcome my dear. I am surprised and pleased that the escort service has sent a Native American for me." Koldo then walked toward the bed, with the young woman behind him. He said, "What is your name darling?"

The beautiful Native American girl said, "Susana." As she continued to walk toward Koldo she moved both hands from behind her back to a position in front of her. Her hand held a large, sharp knife. The steel blade of the knife glistened in the bright light of the motel room.

The woman said, "My name is Susan Richards. I have been following you and I know what you did."

As Koldo turned around to see his female guest, Susana thrust the large knife downward into Koldo's head, between the eyes.

Susana said, "And you will pay for killing the man I love, Harold Gatewood." She then proceeded to scalp Koldo in the same fashion she had used on the three men from the Palcer de los Lectores book publishing company.

Chapter 27

Vudu

June 29

HAROLD GATEWOOD HAD NOT REGAINED CONSCIOUSNESS IN THE HOSPITAL. His mind and body had not recovered from their ordeal. After two hours in his room his mind made a slight recovery. Gatewood then saw bright light, a long runnel, and his smiling grandfather motioning for him to join him. In his mind, Gatewood arose from his hospital bed and, smiling, started to walk to toward his grandfather.

In Santo Domingo, the Dominican Republic, a heavy-set woman clad in a long white-colored skirt, bright turquoise-blue-colored blouse, and leather sandals sat by a table. She had placed five cards on the table in a squared-shaped pattern. Only one card in the middle of the square remained to be turned over.

The woman, a vudu soothsayer, who knew Gatewood, was reading the cards to predict his future. She turned over the middle card on the table and said, "There will be death."

Printed by Libri Plureos GmbH in Hamburg, Germany